DOOMED
BY
Blooms

DOOMED
BY
Blooms

A Josie Posey Mystery

ANNA *St.* JOHN

Chapter One

My palms were damp as I gripped the steering wheel, and I knew it wasn't from the blistering August heat. Most summer days I drove with my little red VW convertible top down and coasted through the village without a care. Something was wrong. During my stellar career as a crime reporter turned crime solver, I came face-to-face with dozens of bad guys. I never flinched. Not once.

Now, my heart raced over a puff piece about a ballerina.

The day began routinely enough. It was early when I let my fluffy sheepdog Moe outside, but the August sun already scorched the begonias in the huge patio pots that lined my deck. I splashed the shrubs with water before I poured my morning coffee, dressed in navy capris and a striped cotton blouse, and hurried through breakfast.

I had spent twenty years as a crime reporter for the *Kansas City Star,* but the ballerina's story was my first assignment for *The Village Gazette.* Here, in this lovely Cotswolds-style community, I struggled to find my place. A rocking-chair life was not for me. Instead, at fifty-five, I itched to get back into the action. This morning's interview was a first step.

Our small-town newspaper served a tiny population, and a feature article about a famous ballerina should have been an easy one. I was curious about the rising star who had chosen to quit at such an early age. Thirty-two was the beginning, for most careers. Any novice reporter could write her story. Yet my stomach twisted into knots as I drew closer to my destination.

I inhaled a long, deep breath, then exhaled it slowly.

As I drove, I ticked through my mental checklist: Notepad. Pen. List of

Questions. *Who was I kidding?* I knew why this interview made me sweat. It was my first in a town where everyone knew me. Correction: Where everyone knew everyone, and I was considered a gray-haired meddler. Well-intentioned, perhaps, but obsolete, nevertheless.

People always said, "It must be wonderful to live in such a quaint little town."

They are fascinated to discover English Village, in Sunflower County, Kansas, where tourists flock to see our cobblestone streets, charming cottages, and spired limestone church. "I had no idea it would be so lovely," they say.

They were right, of course. It was a beautiful place. And friendly. But, as a former big-city girl, I discovered life in a small town had its own challenges. Especially as a senior "newbie"—meaning someone over fifty who had lived here less than twenty years. Even my closest friends had suggested it was time to slow down. I sometimes felt they patronized me, tut-tutting and virtually patting me on the head, as though I were a small child unable to comprehend their words.

The drive to Betty Hamilton's secluded cottage was a short one. I guided my little convertiblethrough the winding roads, giving myself a pep talk all the way. I'd named the car "Piper" after a favorite childhood memory, but it also suited her bright red color. I admit the car was a defiant symbol of my refusal to age gracefully, but I felt happy behind the wheel. As I carried on a one-sided conversation to boost my courage, the unrelenting sun and infamous Kansas humidity turned my graying curls to frizz, and my now-wrinkled top clung to my back.

Remembering the trick my grandmother had taught me to overcome the fear of my first classroom speech, I asked myself, "What's the worst that could happen? Will anyone die?"

As a teenager cursed by an active imagination and a smart mouth, I had responded to Grandma Molly's question with an entire list of bad things that might spell disaster. I could lose my voice, drop my note cards, knock over the podium. And what if Danny laughed or Judy whispered and passed notes the way she always did?

My wise grandmother had wrapped me in her arms for a hug. "Josephina, none of those things matter. Do the best you can do. That's all anyone expects. It may not be perfect this time, but you improve with practice. And no one will die if you fail."

I might die of embarrassment, I thought then.

Deep in introspection, I nearly missed the limestone post that marked my turn, the number 4723 discreetly attached below the subtle face of the mailbox. It was the first of a long row of decorative lighted posts leading down the lane. My friend, Nellie, described these quaint markers as "the footlights to the *Hamilton* stage."

A vast green lawn spread itself before me, dotted with delicate pink blooms dancing atop slender stalks. These must be the "Naked Ladies" my editor mentioned when she described the property. The light breeze ruffled through the flowers, making them sway in unison, a choreographed welcome for my eyes alone. A lovely sprawling stone cottage perched like an island in the center of an emerald sea, the ripples of pink blossoms bobbed like waves in the ocean of green around it.

I braked to breathe in the beauty, and a golden goddess of a dog bounded across the grounds to meet me, ears flapping all the way. She wore a polka-dot scarf around her neck and a ruffled bow on top of her curly head—clearly, the household pet was a fashionista. The pooch hovered beside my car, tail wagging, until I opened the door and stepped out to greet her. I knelt to scratch behind her ears. "Hello, girl. What's your name?"

"We call her Tinkerbelle." I looked toward the gruff voice, but with the bright sun directly behind him, I saw only the silhouette of a tall man, ramrod straight, with broad shoulders. Shielding my forehead to get a better look, I squinted into piercing dark eyes set into a ruggedly handsome face. I guessed him to be in his mid-40s. He didn't smile as he spoke.

"I'm Robert Hamilton. You must be the reporter."

I stood, wiped my wet palms on my pants, and reached to shake his hand. "Josephina Posey."

He ignored my outstretched hand and pivoted abruptly. "Follow me, Ms. Posey. My wife was expecting you seven minutes ago."

Rolling my eyes behind his back, I trailed him as we marched up the sidewalk and into the front entrance. Door chimes announced our arrival, and a young woman appeared on the arched threshold. Shimmering in the sunlight, she was a vision of silver and white. Platinum hair fell in waves that framed her alabaster face, and her brilliant blue eyes were mesmerizing.

She wore an ivory linen sundress and silver sandals that accentuated the length of her legs. And she floated there, more like an apparition than an ordinary woman. I heard a gasp, and it took me a moment to realize it had come from me. Then, two things happened simultaneously. Mr. Hamilton stepped to his left, motioning for me to precede him, and Betty Hamilton smiled.

That smile began in her eyes and extended into the curve of her full lips, revealing a mischievous dimple in her right cheek. Her face lit up with a kindness I hadn't felt since my Grandma Molly died. At that moment, I sensed this interview could lead to a fascinating story, and a lasting friendship.

Soon I was comfortably seated across from the dancer in her cheery sunroom, an icy glass of lemonade in front of me, while we chatted as though we were long-lost friends. Her husband kept a watchful eye from his post in a cane chair near the windows. I never saw him turn a page, but he pretended to read a magazine, and we allowed the pretense. Tinkerbelle rested her head on his knee, so I knew the man had a soft spot for the dog.

From my research, I had expected Betty Hamilton to be an ice princess—lovely but arrogant and cool. In the dance world, she was known for her unrelenting quest for excellence—practicing until her toes bled to ensure perfection onstage. She began her career as an apprentice at the age of seventeen and retired suddenly at thirty-two. The audience was drawn to her striking beauty and her haunting grace.

I was prepared to meet a prima donna. Instead, the ballerina was warm and genuine. She agreed to let me record the interview and answered each question with a thoughtful nod and smile. Occasionally, she glanced toward her husband, who remained in the corner, snacking on chips and salsa while he "read." Their eyes would connect, like lovers' do, sharing words unspoken.

Midway through the formal interview, Betty startled me by asking questions about my career as a reporter. She poured us each a second glass of lemonade, and I noticed her every movement was fluid, graceful.

I declined her offer of chips and salsa, and she set a fresh bowl of each on the small table beside her husband. When she turned back toward me, the corners of her lips twitched as she held back a smile.

"Is it true you prefer to write about criminals, Ms. Posey? I'm afraid my story will be terribly dull compared to the murder cases you covered."

"Please, call me Josie. I wrote about crime while I lived in the city. I have retired from all of that now." I fiddled with the pen in my hand, then laid it gently beside my notepad, trying to emulate her poise.

"You are far too modest, Josie. I read you helped the police solve three murder cases in your final year as an investigative reporter. You earned the citizen's award for valor."

I sipped my lemonade, then set the glass on the table. "The department's public relations team was generous with their awards. I think you'll find at least twenty people who received recognition that year." Still, I was flattered she had taken the time to learn about my career.

Betty's eyes sparkled as she shook her finger at me. "I pictured you as a hard-boiled reporter with frown lines etched on your face. Instead, you look wholesome and innocent – a lot like that *Katie Something* who anchors the news specials on television. It's hard to imagine you as a crime-solving superhero."

I nearly choked on my lemonade at her description. "I wish that were true. Look at me. I'm fifty-five. I stand five-foot-three. I'm twenty pounds overweight. And I'm a coward at heart."

Betty wrinkled her forehead as she shot back at me. "What I see is a smart, spunky woman with a bright smile and those natural curls I always wanted."

"What? But your hair is beautiful. It's part of your persona as a prima ballerina." I was stunned at her comment.

Her eyes took on a wistful look. "We all want something we can't have," she said.

"Perhaps that's true. In my teens, I dreamed of becoming a dancer. Doesn't every little girl want to twirl on stage? Unfortunately, I was too short."

We talked for a while about how I had inherited Grandma Molly's estate, bringing me to retire in English Village—the idyllic little town that had first stolen the heart of my beloved grandmother and later captured my own. I had practically grown up here, spending long vacations with my grandmother every summer of my childhood. It seemed a natural place to move when I left the city life.

When Betty asked about pets, I described my sheepdog, Moe, and she motioned toward Tinkerbelle. "Our Labradoodle is never far from Bob's side. There's nothing like the love of a dog."

While I certainly agreed on that point—and I knew I'd be lonely without Moe—I longed for something more to keep me occupied in the sleepy village. I wasn't content to walk my dog and play a weekly game of mahjong with our town's equivalent of the Golden Girls—though I loved every one of them. When I explained how I talked my way into a part-time writing job with *The Village Gazette*, earning the opportunity to interview her, it was Betty's turn to laugh.

"Somehow that doesn't surprise me," she said.

The dancer clasped her hands and leaned in, fixing her brilliant blue eyes on mine. "You and I have a great deal in common. We both left a big stage behind us to start over in a small town."

"I wish I had seen you dance on that stage!"

"Perhaps you will. I'm scheduled to perform a charity ballet later this year. I'll reserve tickets so you can attend." Her husband cleared his throat from across the room, but Betty kept her eyes on mine.

She explained her decision to open Miss Betty's School of Dance as a natural conclusion to her career in one of the nation's top ballet companies. "Teaching is my true calling."

"Some say you left the ballet at the height of your career. You could have danced for a dozen more years."

Her eyes darted toward her husband again. "Those people don't understand the pressures involved in dancing. It's difficult to make friends in a ballet company when the dancers all compete for the spotlight."

During our two-hour interview, I formed judgments about both Hamiltons.

In my mind, the ballerina was everything her husband was not. Betty was engaging; Robert was taciturn. Betty was graceful; Robert was rigid. Betty was cheerful; Robert was moody. I didn't particularly like the guy. He hovered over his wife like a dark cloud, making me wonder what brought them together.

I wrapped up my questions and turned off the recorder, and Betty walked me to her door. She took both my hands in hers. "Josie, we are both transplants to English Village. I'd like to be friends. Let's get to know each other over coffee sometime. Perhaps next week? My husband's marine buddy is in town, so we're busy entertaining him for the next few days."

Although her tone didn't change, there was a surprising urgency in her touch. I was more than twenty years her senior, but I had learned long ago that age had nothing to do with friendship. I squeezed her hands in return. "I would like that."

We stood in the doorway for only a moment before Robert strode down the hall and wrapped an arm around Betty's waist. Walking toward my car, I turned to wave at the couple. For a moment, the slant of the late morning sun cast Robert's shadow across the dancer's face. Then I blinked, and it was gone.

As I shoved the shadow from my mind, another of Grandma Molly's admonitions came into my head: "Don't borrow trouble, Josie." And, except for writing the ballerina's story, I never planned to pry into her problems. But sometimes, we are pulled into trouble when we least expect it.

Chapter Two

As I returned to my car, the summer heat steamed off the pavement and I was positive the egg-frying thing would work, if someone wanted to attempt it. I grabbed a beach towel from my trunk and draped it over Piper's hot driver's seat before I climbed inside, started the car, and switched on the air conditioning. Then I drove across town using only my fingertips to guide the blistering steering wheel until it finally cooled.

I pulled into my friend Sharon's driveway promptly at 12:50 p.m. and hurried up the sidewalk to her front door. Today was Mahjong Day, and Sharon was hosting.

Thelma and Louise met me on the front porch with wet kisses and friendly tail wagging. My friend's perfectly groomed, standard-size poodles would make terrible guard dogs. Opening the unlocked door, I breathed in the mouthwatering scent of peaches and cinnamon. Sharon had been baking, again.

"I'm here." I shouted down the stairway.

Sharon's freckled face smiled up at me. Her short blonde curls and bright eyes gave her an irresistible, impish look. Forget that she was in her late sixties; this woman was born to party. The smallest of the Mahjong Mavens, Sharon claimed to be our ditsy blonde, but she's as smart as they come, with a warm sense of humor and a big heart.

She waved me down the stairs.

"Come join us. We're setting up the table."

A babble of conversation floated upward, wrapping me in the friendly banter we shared every Wednesday at mahjong. I couldn't wait to see these familiar faces and tell them my news.

I walked into the room and raised my arms to get their attention. "Guess what, ladies? I have an announcement."

The three mavens paused their conversations to look in my direction. I laughed at the quizzical expressions on their faces. In that moment, it was easy to imagine them as schoolgirls, growing up together in this small village before they headed off to college.

Both Nellie and Sharon became teachers. And both returned to English Village within a couple of years of each other. Nellie and her husband Tim lived a block away from Sharon and Terry. They raised their families side by side, as neighbors on the same street.

Kate had ventured farther away from the village, and for a longer time. After high school, she joined the military and earned college degrees in both law and accounting – from Harvard, no less. She spent years in the United States Marine Corps before she retired and returned home to English Village. Although she had a long history with Sharon and Nellie from their school days together, she had joined the Mahjong Mavens more recently, like me.

Nellie Nester tucked her stylish salt-and-pepper bob behind her right ear, like she always did when she stood up from preparing the game table. She rolled her eyes at me and moaned. "What are you getting us into now? I'm almost afraid to ask."

"Wait a minute. Let's give the woman a chance to speak." Kate spoke up, and the ladies looked in her direction. Our self-designated leader and rule interpreter, the stately retired marine, easily commanded attention. Her eyes twinkled in amusement as she added a not-so-subtle punchline. "We all know Josie doesn't *intend* to involve us in adventures. She stumbles into them, and we follow along."

Somehow, I lost control of the conversation as the lively seniors talked over each other. Nellie was the most adventurous of the mavens — always the first to try something new. Now, she stepped closer to get my attention.

"Remember last month when you convinced us to wear disguises and follow that stranger around town?" Nellie said, her dark eyes shining. "That was so much fun."

"Sure it was." Kate threw her hands in the air. "Right up to the point where you and Josie had him trapped in the alley, and he pulled a weapon on you. If Sharon and I hadn't come racing around the corner so fast her wig flew off, he might have shot us all."

I laughed at Kate's description. "Hold on, ladies. This story gets bigger every time you tell it. As you know, there was no gun. He pulled his phone from his pocket 'cause he couldn't believe his eyes and wanted to get a picture of the four women tailing him."

Nellie grinned back at me. "Okay, but I still like the way Kate tells it. And we did round up a bad guy,"

"We did," I agreed. "And even though Chief Marshall grumbled about our involvement, he appreciated our help catching that car thief. We knew the man was 'Trouble-with-a-capital-T' the moment he walked into the café. But the whole thing only lasted an hour. And I didn't make anyone wear a disguise. Sharon had the wig in her car, and the rest of us couldn't wait to put on those gardening hats from Nellie's trunk."

During the short time I'd known these three women, we had joined forces to keep an eye on our village—similar to a neighborhood watch program, only better. We reported a few suspicious characters to the police chief and pretended we were crime solvers, like I had been in the city. It was easy to spot strangers in the small town. The incident with the car thief was the only one that resulted in an arrest, but we were convinced it wouldn't be the last.

The Mahjong Mavens had also worked together on a few community service projects that were more ambitious than I anticipated when I started them. Together, we had initiated a village food pantry and started a weekly Story Hour at the local library. The four of us had plenty of time on our hands, and we weren't afraid to tackle something new.

My grandmother used to say I didn't know when to let a sleeping dog lie. It was true, I suppose. Asking questions and solving problems came naturally to me. During my childhood, this curiosity earned me the nickname "Nosy Josie." When I became a crime reporter, it resulted in a promotion, although it sometimes placed me a little too close to danger.

After they first learned of my former career, my mahjong friends demanded story after story about the bad guys I had helped capture. And that's when we formed our unofficial posse. Most of the mavens wouldn't admit it, but they loved a good adventure.

Now, I regained their attention with a question. "Don't you want to hear the latest?"

Quickly, my best friends in the world gathered around me. I smiled at their eagerness. "Let me assure you this announcement requires no effort from you and creates no risks for any of us. I finally found the perfect part-time job. I will be writing a weekly column for *The Village Gazette,* and I started today—with an interview of Betty Hamilton."

"The ballerina who opened the School of Dance next to the pet store?" Sharon smiled at me over the pitcher of water she was pouring into a glass. The hostess of our group, and our favorite baker, she had a saucy attitude that kept us laughing. "You're right. That's a perfect use of your time. You can ask all the questions you want."

Nellie nodded, her silver earrings dangling below her perfect bob. "Agreed. I've heard Betty has a mysterious past. I can't wait to read all about her."

Kate wrapped an arm around my shoulders. She stood an even five foot eight in her flats and was as slender as a twig. I was a good five inches shorter and outweighed her by twenty pounds. Her silver hair curved around her oval face; my unruly curls were long enough to pull into a tight ponytail on hot days like this one, graying temples and all. Now, my friend peered into my eyes from behind fashionable pewter frames. "This is an opportunity to use that natural curiosity of yours without putting yourself in danger."

Since I trailed them by a decade, all the mavens treated me like a little sister. I tried to accept their admonitions graciously.

"Yes, I know. It will be fun to learn more about some interesting characters in our little town. I shouldn't be able to get into any trouble sitting at my computer, right?"

Nellie slipped the game dice into my hand. "Roll 'em, Nosy Josie. You can do whatever you want the rest of the week, but it's mahjong on Wednesdays."

The chatter turned to business as we devoted full attention to our games. There was always good-natured conversation around the mahjong table, but this group of older women was far more competitive than any of us wanted to admit. It was a good thing we didn't play for money. Bragging rights were enough to keep us coming back every week.

The Chinese tile game always reminded me of home, in the suburbs near Kansas City. My mother played it with her friends for years. When my sisters and I were still small, she taught us to play, too. We cradled the ivory tiles, rubbing our fingers over the etched dragons and flowers, learning to match them to the strange-sounding suits – white dragons with Dots, red dragons with Craks, green dragons with Bams. The first time I successfully collected all fourteen tiles in a pattern that matched a hand on the game card, I jumped from my seat. "I did it!"

"Don't forget to lay the tiles on the top of your display rack," my mother said. "Then, shout 'mahjong!'"

I danced around the table, swishing the game card in the air like a sparkler on the Fourth of July. "Mahjong! Mahjong!"

While other families played Monopoly or card games over the holidays, we spent hours enjoying mahjong. I've played the game for over fifty years and have never tired of it. Every year, we ordered new cards from the National Mah Jongg League. Although the tiles were the same, the formation of the winning hands changed each year.

Every spring, we anticipated receiving the new cards, bringing freshness to the game. Kate sorted through her tiles, frowning. "I'm ready for some new hands. This card hardly uses any flowers, and I have six of them."

Sharon positioned several tiles on the tray in front of her. She always looked fabulous, but today she wore a gossamer summer top that reminded me of fresh lemonade. She raised her huge blue eyes to look across the table at Kate. "We're barely into the year with these. I like the new cards."

"That's because you're winning," Nellie said, waving her card to emphasize her point.

"Only today," Sharon replied. "Usually, I'm the biggest loser."

Kate made the sign of an "L" on her own forehead. "Ladies, I own the Loser title. If you look at the book, you'll see I have lost more games than the rest of you combined."

The infamous spiral notebook contained our record of winners and losers from the last few years. It rested now on Sharon's countertop. As far back as I could remember, no one ever looked at the scores from previous weeks.

Kate sighed and surveyed her tiles again. "If we could create our own hands, I would do one with all flowers and winds."

Nellie clasped her hands and raised an eyebrow at Kate. "No whining. Whose turn is it to discard?" Of the four mavens, Nellie was the most practical. She kept the game on track when the rest of us strayed. She did the same thing with our lives, nudging each of us with unsolicited advice when she felt we needed it—which was often.

The banter continued in much the same fashion each week. Our Mahjong Mavens played a series of games, straight through, from 1:00 to 3:00 p.m. every Wednesday afternoon. We rarely found time for lengthy conversations, yet we shared enough about our lives to become close friends over the years. I was still discovering things the three childhood friends had known about each other for a lifetime, thus the "Miss Nosy" nickname. But I didn't mind. These older ladies had welcomed me into their circle to play a game I had loved since childhood. Mahjong was not a household word in our little community. Few people I met had heard of the game.

My life had changed since I moved into the little cottage in English Village. And it came at the perfect time. The week I retired from my journalism career, Ken, my college sweetheart and husband of thirty-five years, died suddenly from a heart attack. Our sons, Chris and Luke, both lived abroad, leaving me to begin a new life on my own.

The same day I moved to the cottage, I adopted my fluffy Old English sheepdog puppy and named him Moe. Yes, I knew Jo and Moe were rhyming names ready-made for jokes. But I had heard it all before. My mother named me Josephina after her favorite aunt, my great-aunt Josie. By the time I was twelve, I had heard so many "Rosie Josie" and "Nosy Josie" taunts that I switched to "Jo." Then, ironically, I married Ken Posey and became "Josie Posey" for the rest of my married life. As much as I tried to be a "Jo," the rest of the world continued to revert to calling me "Josie."

The Mahjong Mavens were a close-knit group long before I moved to town. Nellie—who we sometimes called Nell—and Sharon had lived near each other for so long they were like sisters. They often volunteered their time to our local Dress for Success organization, coaching women on how to reenter the workforce as they recovered from some terrible situations. Both had retired from teaching careers and were passionate about helping other women succeed.

Kate stayed fit with yoga classes and devoted her spare time to the local food pantry. Every single one of these ladies had a soft spot for others in need, and that's how we became friends. We kept running into each other as community volunteers.

As we began our last game of the day, my cell phone rang. "I'm sorry, ladies. I left it on because the editor of the paper said she would call to see how my interview went. Let me tell her I'll call back in a few."

But before I could relay the message to my editor, Leslie Anderson, she interrupted me in a frantic voice an octave higher than normal. "Jo, the ballerina's husband is dead."

"What? When?"

"Betty found him face down in the flowers, foaming at the mouth. Hurry. Get back over there. They think he was murdered."

By the time I ended the call, the Mahjong Mavens were on red alert.

"Something terrible happened, didn't it, Josie?" Nell's eyes bored into mine.

I stared back, my mind whirling.

"Betty's husband is dead!"

My heart raced with adrenalin. The puff piece was now a crime story.

And then I realized something more important. My new friend was certain to be a suspect.

I needed to do more than write the story. I had to solve the murder.

Chapter Three

On my way home, I talked again with Leslie, who pushed me to jump on the story. She knew my history as a crime reporter and considered it a stroke of good fortune that I had established a relationship with the ballerina that very morning. She wanted an investigative report; and she wanted it now. While I was happy to oblige, I needed time to process the news of Bob's death.

Leslie insisted I return to Betty's immediately, to question her. Without thinking, I circled the block and retraced my route from the morning. Turning again at the limestone pillar that marked the lane to her property, I guided Piper to the spot where the road curved; but the place was crowded with police vehicles, red and blue lights flashing. A kind young officer took my card and turned me away.

The rebuke stung. In the city, authorities recognized my face and would have waved me through to the crime scene. I was the reporter who convinced Vinnie "The Rat" Ratoni to talk about his murder-for-hire scheme, which effectively removed Kansas City's top drug lord and established Ratoni as the new King of Cocaine. The conspiracy, and my story reporting it, landed Ratoni a murder sentence in the Lansing Penitentiary. Earlier, when the Angel of Darkness serial killer sent letters to the *Kansas City Star*, I assisted the FBI in tracking the thumb drive to a church in nearby Lenexa—a major break in the case, leading to the arrest of the assistant pastor.

When I wrote for the *Kansas City Star*, law enforcement officers in high places welcomed my theories. Here, I had no credibility. Worse, the police chief saw me as a meddling intruder. That realization brought doubts to my mind. It had been over three years since my last big headlines resulted in the successful arrest and conviction of a murderer. I had written nothing since my husband died—taking my time to overcome my grief and settle into English Village.

What if I have forgotten how?

Sighing, I pulled into my garage and stepped inside the cottage to find Moe waiting at the door. I set my bag on the kitchen counter, tucked my keys into my pocket, and grabbed the leash from its hanger. The sun was relentless as Moe and I took the brief walk I had promised him, but the exercise helped clear my mind. We made our favorite circle, striding the length of the sidewalk from my cottage to the historic park, around the village namesake Hank English statue, and back again.

By the time we returned, I had a plan. Pulling my interview notes from my handbag, I settled into the cool quiet of the cottage. With a tall glass of iced tea on the end table and the tape recorder at my side, I delved into the details of Betty Hamilton's life. An hour later, I had piles of index cards scattered into ragged groupings across the couch. I attached sticky notes to a dozen of them, as reminders to ask more questions. For added inspiration, I turned on my favorite "thinking music." Jim Brickman's soothing piano solos flowed around the paper-mountain havoc, and my late-husband Ken smiled at me from his framed photo on the mantle.

Moe sat at my feet, his head resting on my knee while I studied the scribbled words, searching for clues. Soon, the couch was completely covered in papers, and I had circled various names with a red marker. Could any of these people have killed the ballerina's husband?

As I worked, I created a list for the mahjong ladies to review. They knew everyone. Nothing happened in English Village that one of my mahjong friends didn't know about. At least, I hoped that was true. I was counting on them to replace the network of informants I'd relied on as a crime reporter in the city. If I could do the research and enlist their help, I was sure we could get the murder solved. This was a small town, with nowhere for a killer to hide.

The circumstances of Bob Hamilton's death were fuzzy. This morning, he lounged in the screened-in sunroom while I interviewed Betty twenty feet away. By one in the afternoon, he was convulsing in the field of Naked Ladies. While I played mahjong, he fought for his life. Within a few hours, he was gone.

According to my *Gazette* editor, who had her own sources around town, the ballerina's husband had several enemies. Robert (Bob) Hamilton was a former US Marine and hard-nosed on nearly everything. His mechanic complained about him; the local dog walker disliked him; even the farmer who leased his property had argued with him.

Since I had been the last "outsider" to see Bob Hamilton alive in his home, I wasn't surprised when Chief Marshall called to announce he was on his way to my cottage. In fact, I was at the top of his list for an interview. The chief was a solid, small-town police officer. He built a strong department, trained his team well, and earned the respect of the community.

I liked him. In fact, I considered him a friend. He was supportive of my food bank idea, and I reciprocated when he needed volunteers for a community bicycle safety event. But I knew from experience he would not welcome unsolicited crime-solving help from reporters, especially retired, big-city journalists like me.

If I hoped to solve this murder, I would have to tiptoe around Chief Marshall.

I answered the familiar knock of the chief's firm hand and opened the door wide for him to enter. "Come in, Chief." I smiled and motioned toward my cluttered kitchen island. "Could I get you something? Coffee? Water?"

"Coffee. Two sugars, no milk."

While I poured his cup of coffee, the chief stood looking at me. His starched uniform was rumpled, and sweat stains marked his armpits. The chief was a large man. He'd been a star running back on the local football team during high school, earning a full university scholarship. People still remembered him when he returned home with his shiny new diploma and a degree in criminal justice. He paid his dues as a traffic cop for a few years. The football fans still loved him. They elected him police chief the first time he campaigned for the job. He was only thirty—the youngest in the state, at the time—and the only black chief in the county. Now, at thirty-eight, he was one of three.

Moe sauntered toward him and sat, raising his paw in welcome. Chief Marshall broke into a smile and shook the dog's hand. "You teach him that?"

"Yes, but he only does it when he likes the visitor. I guess you passed the test."

The weary man accepted a seat at my kitchen island. Moe laid down at his feet.

"I won't keep you long, Jo. I'm here to find out what you know about the Hamiltons. Let's start with your observations from this morning. Did you see anything unusual when you were out to their place?"

"I'm sorry you're faced with a suspicious death in town. But are you sure it's a murder? Couldn't it be a heart attack or a tropical virus or something?"

"Take my word for it. This was most likely a murder." The chief's serious brown eyes turned black as he stared into mine. Small beads of sweat gathered above his ebony brow, and he leaned his elbows heavily onto the cool marble surface of the island.

"Bob Hamilton was poisoned. He ate or drank something that caused severe seizures, followed by convulsions that stopped his heart. The coroner hasn't completed his report yet, but he predicts the poison was administered around lunchtime. Bob died at the hospital by 2:30 p.m. His wife was by his side."

"Poison. I can't believe anyone would do that, even if they didn't like him."

"You're far too trusting. Bad things happen. Even in our little village."

"Maybe he was allergic to his lunch?"

The chief shook his head slowly. "The doctor said Bob ate simple meals and rarely tried new foods. It would be highly unusual for him to have a sudden allergic reaction to the foods he ate regularly. We'll find out soon."

I sipped my coffee and considered the chief's comment. "He seemed like a man who liked predictable routines," I said.

"Let's get back to your morning interview with Betty. Tell me what you learned." He pulled a pen and a small spiral notepad from his pocket.

Gathering a stack of notecards from my living room, I returned to sit across from the chief. "I don't think there's anything here to help you, but I'll share what I know." I read parts of the dancer's biography out loud while the chief listened.

"Betty Lou Hamilton was born and raised in New York City. She studied dance and choreography at the Center for Ballet and the Arts, through New York University, and received The Victoria S. Glickman Fellowship for Women in Dance—which is a big deal." I waited for his response, but Chief Marshall said nothing.

Waving my notes in front of his face, I pointed to an article I had printed from the Internet. "It's a fellowship designed for women choreographers and composers that promote broader gender equity in the field of dance. These fellows work on projects that expand the way we think about the history, practice, and performance of dance."

The chief sighed. "I got it. She's a real ballerina. What else?"

"Well, she's always had that platinum blond hair. It's natural. Her favorite flower is the Naked Lady, which makes perfect sense because it looks a lot like a dancer, with those gorgeous pink petals perched on top of the long green stem. Have you seen the field in front of the Hamiltons' home? It's filled with Naked Ladies. Oh my gosh. That's where he died, isn't it?" I could hear myself jabbering, and the chief's expression was grim.

"I don't think you understand what I'm looking for. What about her husband? When did they meet? Were they close? Was her marriage rocky?"

I rolled my eyes at him and shrugged my shoulders. "How would I know? I'm a reporter, not a marriage counselor. You think she might have killed her own husband? She's a dancer, for goodness sakes."

"It's common knowledge. The spouse is always a suspect. Maybe she was unhappy leaving the big city and relocating to our tiny village where she's stuck teaching five-year-olds to point their toes."

"Betty seemed thrilled with her studio here. She talked about her summer classes and the kids. She loved teaching. And Bob sat there, listening to everything she said."

The chief shook his head. I could hear the disappointment in his voice. "I'm going there now to take a detailed statement from the woman. We'll get to the bottom of it. It could be they were running away from the city—or someone in it."

I grabbed my notepad and started scribbling.

"What are you doing?"

"Making more notes, so I can help you find the killer, of course. Besides, my editor wants me to do an in-depth story on the murder."

He took my pad and leaned toward me. "You will not, under any circumstances, get involved in this case. Whoever the murderer is, he or she will not hesitate to protect their identity. I don't want you to become the next victim. Don't talk to anyone about Mr. Hamilton's death. Keep your distance but let me know if you think of anything else that might be helpful."

I stood and squared my shoulders before I spoke. "First, the mavens already know about Robert Hamilton's death, so it's too late to warn me about keeping it quiet. And second, I plan to ask a few questions around town. It's part of my job, Chief. I intend to write a news story for the *Gazette*."

He stomped to the door without speaking, then turned to scowl at me.

"You and your posse of biddies need to stay out of my investigation."

My mouth dropped open, and I struggled to find words. "Biddies? Did you call my friends 'biddies'? Do you even know what that means?"

"You bet I do. I grew up on a farm. I've seen what happens when a brood of old hens goes pecking around where they don't belong."

"Old?"

"Come on, Jo. You know what I meant."

"You take that back, or I'm calling Lorene."

"You're going to tattle on me to my wife?" I saw the hint of a smile at the corner of his mouth. Lorene was small in stature, but she ran the Cozy Cups Cafe with a firm hand, and our mavens admired her spunk. I knew she could put the chief in his place.

"If that's what it takes," I added.

He spread his hands in surrender. "I apologize. I can't stop you from doing your job, but reporting a story differs from investigating a crime. I trust you will share with me any important details you may discover. And don't mention the murder to anyone else until tomorrow, when I've had time to prepare an official statement."

"Is that a command or a request?"

"It's a request. Please." He raised an eyebrow and smiled ever-so-slightly. I nodded but refused to smile back.

The chief closed the door behind himself, and I turned to Moe. "She didn't do it, Moe. I know she didn't. We have to find out who did."

Settling into a chair at the spacious dining room table, I started a new list of potential suspects, jotting information beside each of them. The chief told me to let him know if I learned anything else. Obviously, that meant he wanted me to keep thinking. I went through my short list and fired off a series of texts to the Mahjong Mavens. They were perfectly situated to help rank the suspects, and they already knew about the murder, so I wasn't violating the chief's directive.

First, I wanted to know more about Bob Hamilton. Betty said he had been in the military. They met at a Marine Ball after one of her performances in the city. One of his buddies was in town for a reunion. He was probably staying at the Philbrook Bed and Breakfast. I knew which of the Mahjong Mavens to call—former U.S. Marine, Kate Arnold. She often stopped by the Philbrook for dinner.

Kate picked up on the third ring. "Hi, Josie, what's up?"

I phrased my request carefully. Kate was a stickler for following the chain of command and would not knowingly go around the chief.

"Chief Marshall left here a few minutes ago, and he's asked me to do some quiet investigating on the ballerina's husband. Do you think you could help?"

I explained what I needed. "If you could stop by the inn for dinner, maybe you will run into the marine buddy who came to visit this week. You don't have to approach him unless you see an opportunity. I thought if you're having dinner near him, and you mention that Bob Hamilton died, you could see if you get a reaction. But don't say it's murder, because we can't mention that part, yet."

"Honestly, Josie, this sounds like the very thing Chief Marshall would tell you not to do." Kate's tone conveyed her doubts about the assignment. "Are you sure he approved this little exploration of yours?"

"Well, not exactly. But he told me to let him know if I came up with anything. And Betty mentioned that Bob's buddy was in town, so it seems logical we could learn a little more about the guy."

I paused, deciding whether to tell her the chief's comment about our mavens. "He called us a posse of biddies."

She gasped at the "B-word," and I could hear a new determination in her response. "I've got this. I already planned to stop by the inn this evening. Not for dinner, but for a slice of Sharon's delicious peach pie they serve for dessert. I'll let you know if I run across any military types in the dining room."

"Thank you, thank you."

As soon as Kate ended the call, Moe and I headed out for a brief evening walk, my mind churning with ideas about how Bob Hamilton could have been poisoned and who would have done such a terrible thing.

Biddies, indeed. Our mavens would show the chief what a brood of old hens could do.

Chapter Four

The late summer sun was several hours from setting as Moe and I turned toward the park. This was our favorite walking path, and I let him take the lead. He trotted happily past the historic little blacksmith shop toward the beautiful gazebo where so many young couples were married.

My mind reeled from the news of Bob Hamilton's death, and I took a few moments to rest on a bench inside the shaded gazebo. Moe sat at my feet as I leaned my head back to study the intricate lattice overhead. The solid framework of the structure was comforting, somehow. It fit together like a complicated puzzle, leaving no dangling shapes or unanswered questions. The roof had been constructed to provide shade for those occupying the space below. It performed the task without surprises.

I longed for simple, logical answers to Mr. Hamilton's death, but they eluded me. Did someone plan the man's murder as carefully as the builder had designed this gazebo? Had they considered the consequences for the wife he left behind? Who would do such a thing? And why? My anxiety level increased as I considered how alone Betty must feel at this very moment. I had lost my own husband quite suddenly, so I could imagine her disbelief. Her world would never be the same again. I wanted to go and comfort her, but I knew I shouldn't.

A familiar wave of apprehension and nausea washed over me, and I leaned forward to place my head between my knees. Sweet Moe whined and leaned against my leg to comfort me. Every time I thought I had moved past the sadness of my own husband's death, something happened to transport me back to that day. At least I had learned how to deal with the nausea. I could be thankful for that.

After a few deep breaths, I rose from the bench and continued our walk. Moe and I stopped by the water fountain designed for humans and their pets to share. While Moe lingered for great gulps of water at the ground-level water bowl, I sipped from the bubbling water positioned for adults. I turned to study the centerpiece of the park: a fifteen-foot-tall bronze sculpture of our city's namesake, Henry English. It made me smile every time I read the plaque at its base. Here we were, in the middle of Sunflower County, Kansas, living in a place called English Village. And it was named after a British man who had never set foot in America.

"Listen to this, Moe." I called the dog to my side, and he listened as I read. "Henry Nolan 'Hank' English was born July 5, 1883, and died March 31, 1919. He was the son of a Welsh father and a French mother, an artist in the Welsh Movement, and a prominent soldier in World War I." I scratched the fur on Moe's neck. "What do you think of that? "Moe cocked his head and looked up at me happily, his tongue lolling out the side of his mouth.

"I agree. This guy must have been something special," I said. "He was thirty-five when he died, but someone admired him enough to memorialize him a long way from his homeland. Quite a story, right?"

The door to the blacksmith shop slammed open, and a tall, gangly man wearing a protective leather apron stepped out. I watched from the corner of my eye as he strode toward the water fountain, his long legs closing the distance between us. I guessed Harvey Jacobs to be around forty-eight, but he looked younger—with reddish hair, brilliant blue eyes, and a lopsided smile that lit up his face. Wiping his forehead with a handkerchief, he teased, "You talking to yourself again, Jo?"

"Of course not. I'm talking to Moe. He's the best listener."

"That's a fact." Harvey tucked the handkerchief into his pocket and walked toward me. "I had to get outside to cool off a bit. The only place that's hotter than this sun is the inside of that blacksmith shop. Normally, I would wait till late evening to get started in there, but with the Summer's End Festival coming up, I must work a few extra hours to get my stuff ready to sell."

"I was out of town last year," I said, "so this will be my first time for the festival. I'm not sure what to expect."

Harvey shook his head slowly. "You won't believe how many tourists we attract. Folks come from everywhere to honor Hank English, shop at the crafts booths and enjoy the end of summer. Food trucks will circle the park. And this year, little kids from Betty's School of Dance will be performing routines in the gazebo. With all those tiny tutus on display, it's going to be a sight to see."

When he mentioned Betty, my mind raced to Bob's death, and I froze. I stood speechless, staring into Harvey's kind eyes for several moments before I blurted it out: "Betty Hamilton is a suspect in her husband's murder. The chief is over there right now, and I don't know what's going to happen." Tears streamed down my face, and I told Harvey I had interviewed the ballerina this morning.

"I saw her with Bob. They seemed happy," I added, "except I sort of thought he was a little controlling. There was tension between them. Then the chief called and said Bob was dead. Murdered. He thinks I should know something, but I don't. I really don't. I wish I did." Suddenly I was babbling; my body shook uncontrollably.

Harvey placed his hands on my shoulders and squeezed them to steady me. I inhaled the earthy smell of his leather apron. He was so close I could see his biceps taut against the fabric of his shirt. "Whoa. I'm sorry to hear about Mr. Hamilton, but it's not your fault." He bent down to look me directly in the eyes. Speaking slowly, he said exactly what I needed to hear: "Jo. Calm down. It's okay. Nobody expects you to know more than you do."

And when he said it, I believed it. My heart stopped racing, and the trembling eased. Embarrassed, I stepped back from Harvey and shook my head. "I'm sorry to fall apart like that. I guess it all hit me at once. It hasn't seemed real, and now it does. The chief left my house to go back over to Betty's. I'm sure he will figure it all out."

"No worries." Harvey studied my face and tucked his hands into his pockets. "It's a weighty burden to be one of the last people to see someone alive. I'd be concerned if you didn't experience some symptoms of shock. And it's not unusual to have a delayed reaction."

"Thanks, Harv." I gave him a tentative smile. "I wasn't supposed to say anything about the murder. I told the chief I'd help find the killer, but I'd appreciate it if you could keep it to yourself until the word gets out through the village grapevine."

"I'm not leaving the blacksmith shop until at least midnight. I even packed a sandwich for my dinner break. Your news is safe with me."

We said our goodbyes, and Moe and I continued our walk across the park. The steady pace of his paws helped to calm my mind. It seemed impossible that this morning I was happily chatting with Betty while her husband watched from his chair nearby. So much had changed in a few short hours.

I wondered what would happen with the investigation, and I couldn't shake the feeling that I might be able to help the ballerina clear her name. That's when I decided to stop by her house—the chief's wishes could wait. I worried that she was alone, facing this tragedy—not only the loss of her husband, but the possibility that she was a suspect in his murder. I wanted to tell her how sorry I was to hear about Bob's death. And I hoped I could be a shoulder for her to lean on.

I imagined my mother's voice telling me not to go. It wasn't my place. Let the police do their job. As usual, I ignored the warning. Moe and I turned left at the edge of the park and strolled down the five blocks of our tiny Main Street on our way home. We passed the Curiosity Shop and the bank before we came to Miss Betty's School of Dance. It was probably my overactive imagination, but I could have sworn that I saw a glimmer of movement behind the ornate glass panel that framed the front door.

Then, Moe's nose twitched, and I, too, caught a whiff of a hot dog from Mr. Nutter's food truck at the end of the block. I had to hustle to keep up with Moe.

The elderly food vendor wore blue jeans that sagged over his slim frame and a plaid cotton shirt. I'd yet to see him in a T-shirt. For Mr. Nutter's generation, a short-sleeved button-down shirt was the definition of casual. He greeted Moe warmly. "Welcome back, boy. You know I've always got a few scraps ready and waiting for you, buddy." Stepping out of the truck, he set a bowl of water and a paper plate with several bits of hot dog onto the sidewalk.

"What, no napkin?" I placed my hands on my hips as I teased the old man. "This guy loves coming here. You've made a friend for life."

"Happy to have the two of you as customers." Mr. Nutter smiled and watched Moe gobble his treat. He shoved his straw hat back farther on his head, wisps of gray hair sticking out around his ears. "This retirement project has turned into a booming business."

"I hear you. When you're accustomed to working hard and fast, it's a challenge to figure out how to slow down. Tonight, we're going to add to your coffers. Moe and I have decided to dine out. Or, I should say, we're going to order here and take it home with us. Ordering out but dining in. Does that make sense?"

"It does to me." Mr. Nutter laughed as he climbed back into the food truck. "Could I interest you in some barbecued beef tips and a loaded baked potato? It might be a little more nutritious than a foot-long hot dog."

Fifteen minutes later, Moe dozed on his favorite rug under the dining room table while I finished off the last of the beef tips. As he slept, I slipped quietly out the front door and drove toward Betty Hamilton's home.

Chapter Five

On the way to Betty's, I had second thoughts about dropping in unannounced. I pulled to the side of the road and dialed her number instead. She picked up quickly, and I heard her sadness. "H-hello." There was a catch in her voice.

"It's Josie," I said. "I wanted to tell you how very sorry I am for your loss. Chief Marshall told me about what happened to Bob. And, while I know—I mean, I can't possibly know how you are feeling right now. But could I come by and sit with you for a while? I lost my husband suddenly, too. We don't have to talk, unless you want to. But maybe it would be good to have someone with you for a bit?"

She surprised me with her calm reply. "Yes, Josie. I think I would like that. Our pastor is visiting tomorrow, but that seems like a long time from now. Could you bring Moe?"

It was as simple as that. In the end, I went back for Moe and called Nellie to go along with us. She brought one of the delicious casseroles she always stashed in her freezer and one of Sharon's pies. We knocked at Betty Hamilton's door within the hour. For a quiet woman, she had a lot to say. Mostly, Nell and I listened and nodded.

We each ate a piece of Sharon's peach pie, and for a moment, I was distracted by its sweet perfection. I told Betty and Nell about a conversation I had with Sharon. "Did you ever think of baking as a stress reliever? Sharon said when she follows the directions of a recipe she is as focused as a scientist. She concentrates on each step, and it takes her mind off everything else. For her, it's relaxing."

"It wouldn't be for me." Betty tossed her long platinum blonde hair and waved her hands as she spoke. "I tried to bake a birthday cake for Bob once. It had a crack down the center so wide I couldn't get the cake out of the pan without it falling apart."

"What did you do?" I asked.

"What could I do? I filled the crack with frosting. Bob scooped the pieces into a bowl and ate it with a spoon." Her eyes teared at the memory. "He claimed it was his favorite way to eat cake."

"He must have been a kindhearted man," Nellie said.

"He…was." Betty stumbled over the past tense. "After he learned I loved a certain kind of flower, he began planting them for me. He even built a small greenhouse so I could enjoy them year-round. A lot of people never saw that side of him. They thought he was a hard-headed marine with a chip on his shoulder."

I put my hand over hers on the table. "They didn't know the man who planted Naked Ladies for you and ate your broken cake."

We had such a great visit with Betty, it didn't occur to me that Chief Marshall would think we were meddling into his investigation. That is, not until I ran into him at the village library the next morning.

"Ms. Posey, may I have a word?" He motioned me to join him near the computer lab toward the back of the reference section.

I knew right away I was in trouble. The chief never called me "Ms. Posey." No one did. I'm either Josie or Jo. Occasionally someone called me "JoJo," in front of the children at the library. But I was never, ever, Ms. Posey.

I fidgeted a bit, rearranging some books that had fallen sideways on the shelf. Finally, in my hushed "library voice," I said, "You wanted a word?" I looked up at him innocently. "How can I help, Chief?"

"You can help by not helping." The chief spoke sternly, with a glare in his eyes. "Didn't I tell you specifically to stay out of my investigation?"

"As I recall, you said not to try to solve the murder on my own," I answered quickly, stretching my back to reach my full height. "And I haven't."

The chief's eyes bored into mine. "I said you were not—under any circumstances—to get involved. And yet you went to see Betty Hamilton last night."

"How do you know that?"

The chief stood with his hands on his hips, looking at me.

"Well, anyway, that wasn't interfering in an investigation," I continued. "I know how it feels to lose a husband. She needed to talk. I didn't go alone or ask any murder-related questions. I took a friend and went for a brief visit to let Betty know she wasn't alone."

"And did you learn anything interesting?"

I shook my head enthusiastically as I recalled our conversation. "We learned so much about the ballerina and her husband. What a beautiful love story she shared. It made me wish I had known them both for much longer than I did."

The chief sighed loudly. "You may be the most exasperating woman I have ever met. Listen carefully. I do not want you to visit Betty Hamilton. I do not want you to research her life or talk to her friends. I want you to go about your regular life and avoid my murder investigation. Can you do that?"

"Of course I can." I huffed at the tone of his voice. "But you know I have helped solve murders before. And part of my regular life includes gathering information for a story on this murder. You did say I could tell you if I heard anything that might be helpful."

"I did say that." He nodded slowly.

"Good. Because Nellie and I are making a list of things you might find interesting. She's typing it up nice and neat, and we will drop it off for you this afternoon."

"I give up," the chief said dramatically, raising his hands in surrender. "Bring me your notes. But promise me, from now on, you will stop digging into this case."

I answered by grinning back at him. This was going better than I had hoped. We'd see what he thought of our Mahjong Mavens after Nellie, and I handed him solid leads to the murder. "See you this afternoon."

I finished the children's story time around eleven. It was something I did every Tuesday and Thursday morning at the library, and it kept me grounded.

I loved selecting the books and planning discussions or activities they would enjoy. But mostly, I looked forward to their questions and comments. The children always helped me see familiar stories in a new way.

Nellie and I met for a quick lunch at the Cozy Cups Café, the casual coffee and tea shop directly across the street from Miss Betty's School of Dance. The place attracted all kinds of people—from the cops who stopped in on their breaks to the business owners who worked nearby. We invited Kate to join us, and she invited Sharon. I figured we might as well have the whole gang on hand. The Mahjong Mavens would have things sorted out in no time.

Nellie is a take-charge kind of person. I let her call the meeting to order. Tucking her perfect gray bob behind her right ear, she began a detailed report on our visit with Betty.

"She's truly a special woman. She has a tremendous résumé as a professional dancer, and yet she's here in our little village, teaching children to dance. I am so impressed by her decision to leave the big city behind—although I'm still wondering about what prompted her to give up her career."

"Cut to the chase," Sharon interjected. She looked lovely in pink today, but there was nothing girly about her attitude. Leaning closer to Nellie, she demanded an answer to the question on everyone's mind. "Did she kill Bob?"

"No way," Nellie blurted out. "Absolutely not. She loved him. But there *was* another man in her life."

"What?" Sharon interrupted, bouncing in her seat with anticipation. Her chic blonde hairstyle took ten years off her true age. "Who? When?"

Nellie smiled, enjoying the suspense. "There was a guy—a former dance partner. And he was deeply in love with her. His name was Michael. He studied to be a botanist, but his first love was ballet. Defying his father's wishes, Michael dropped out of his prestigious university to pursue a career in dance and choreography. He met Betty. And the rest is history."

"Wait a minute." It was Kate's turn to interrupt. She sat upright, her posture indicating her no-nonsense style. "I'm not following you. What history? She's married to Bob."

Nellie spread her arms wide. "If you'll listen, I'll tell the story. Michael became Betty's dance partner. He fell in love with her. But her heart belonged to Bob. So, they parted ways. Betty and Bob moved here to English Village. Michael returned to the university to finish his degree in botany. But..."

"But, what?" Kate prompted. She ran her hand through her short silver curls impatiently.

"But he never stopped loving her. And he sent her flowers every week, even after she married Bob."

"Every week?" Sharon's voice shrieked, the pink ruffles billowing around her neck. "That's a lot of flowers."

"Yes. Every single week, for the last ten years." Nellie grinned at the shocked expressions surrounding her. "And he still comes to visit often. Isn't that romantic?"

"I don't know, ladies," Kate said, rubbing her temples. "It borders on stalking."

Nellie nodded. "Exactly. And that's why we are listing Mr. Michael Wilson, the botanist, as a suspect in the murder."

"What about the marine?" Sharon wondered aloud. She turned her freckled face to Kate. "Did you see him last night?"

"The marine didn't do it," Kate answered, military-style, in clipped phrases with no hesitation. "I met him. I liked him. And, let's face it, a marine would use a gun or his muscles if he wanted to kill someone. No self-respecting U.S. Marine would stoop to poison as a murder weapon."

I held my pen poised over my notepad, waiting for the next name. "We've got the marine and the botanist. Anyone else as a suspect?" I glanced at Nellie.

Nellie smiled that secret smile of hers. "Yes. We have at least three other suspects."

"Who?" I protested, startled. In my mind, I had only identified one other possibility, and he had no motive. "I don't see anyone else who qualifies."

Nellie shrugged and counted on her fingers. "There's the dog walker who had a crush on Betty. There's the gardener who provided all her fresh produce. And there's the dance apprentice who seemed to spend a lot of time with Bob."

I looked at the three women around me. The mavens were hanging on every word. They didn't look like biddies to me. "We still must do more investigating. These are all names that came up last night when we visited Betty at her home. Nellie and I put our collective intuition to work to read between the lines of what the ballerina shared. Obviously, Nellie is more suspicious than I am."

"Whew, this is complicated." Sharon set her napkin on her lap and picked up her menu. "Let's eat lunch and figure it out later."

I grinned at her. "Agreed."

The mavens were hooked. It was only a matter of time until they poked their noses into the nooks and crannies of the case. I would not mention their involvement when Nellie and I met with the chief this afternoon. He would find out soon enough.

Chapter Six

After our successful introduction of the murder case to the mavens, Nellie and I were on a roll. We couldn't wait to present our theories to the chief and see his reaction. But I had some business of my own to take care of first.

We stopped by the blacksmith shop to thank Harvey for his kindness yesterday. Plus, I'll admit, I wanted to see what he was creating for the Summer's End Festival. Harvey was a businessman by day: he owned and operated the hardware store his grandfather had founded two generations ago. But his true passion was turning metal into works of art. He and two other area artists shared the workspace at the blacksmith shop. One was a glassblower; another was a silversmith. Harvey specialized in iron and steel.

The little blacksmith shop operated like an antique store. They had no regularly posted business hours and rarely opened it to the public. Everyone in English Village knew the three designers spent evenings there, working on their projects. When visitors stopped by, the craftsmen generally encouraged them to come in and watch their progress.

At least twice a year, they sold some of their completed pieces—in the Christmas season and at the Summer's End Festival. The rest of the time, they were focused on commissioned work. Secretly, I hoped I could convince Harvey to let me write about them for our local newspaper. So far, he had shown no interest in publicity for himself, the trio, or the shop.

Harvey's old red pickup was parked out front, and we pulled into the space beside it. As we entered the unlocked shop, we smelled the heat of the open flames, and a rush of hot air burst from the forge. My handsome friend was in his leather apron, bending a thin strip of wrought iron into a delicate curve. Sweat glistened on his face and muscular arms. He grinned up at us as we entered.

"Welcome, ladies. Look over my display table. I'll finish this bend, then I'll take a break to show you around."

While we waited, Nell and I circled a huge table in the center of the room. Nearly every inch was covered with unique wrought iron decorative pieces. The center held practical items, like mug racks and cookbook holders, spaced carefully between candle holders and wall sconces. Around the outside edge, Harvey had arranged artistic wall hangings and a few beautifully intricate mirrors embraced in a latticework of iron. At the very end of the table was a mystery piece covered with lightweight burlap to disguise its shape. Naturally, this was the piece Nell and I wanted most to see. We stood beside it, waiting for Harvey to join us.

"Now I see why you have been spending so much time at the hardware store," Nellie whispered beside me. She motioned to Harvey, who was bending intently over the fire. His biceps stretched against the light fabric of his shirt, and his face glowed from the heat.

"Hush," I nudged her, not so gently. "I have not."

"Well then, you should be," she laughed.

"Should be what?" Harvey took off his gloves and walked over to join our conversation.

"Nothing," I insisted. "Nellie is always telling me what I should or shouldn't do. She has all kinds of great advice." I shot her a warning look, and she smiled innocently, shrugging her shoulders.

My friend extended her hand to Harvey. "I'm Nellie Nester. I haven't said hello since you moved back to the village. But I remember your grandfather and your dad—both keeping the hardware store going for so many years. And, if I'm not mistaken, you played high school basketball with my husband Tim's younger brother, Jimmy Nester."

Harvey smiled and took her hand. "I think you're right. How is Tim?"

"Tim is fine. He finally opened that furniture store he was always talking about. How's your dad?" Nellie asked.

"He's eighty-two, but he doesn't want to stop working. The hardware store is his life. My return has been good for both of us. He works a little less, and I still have time for this crazy hobby of mine." He motioned to the table filled with completed projects.

"We were admiring you. Er, your work," I stammered as Nellie pretended to flex her muscles from behind Harvey's back. "Will all of these be for sale at the festival?"

"Every single one." Harvey walked around the table to stand beside me as he pointed out features of each item. "I've made an assortment to fit different price ranges and interests. But I'd appreciate any advice you ladies can give me on how to best display them."

I glanced toward Nell. "Any ideas, my friend?"

She spoke right up. "Well, these are all beautiful, of course…."

Harvey noticed the pause in her voice. "But?"

"But women need to see how the items will look in their own homes. You should demonstrate that to them. Put candles in the holders and cookbooks on those bookstands. Lean the mirrors up against blocks of wood or hang them from a display wall. Put flowers in the sconces. And, if you have time, take a few pictures of the decorative wall hangings as they would appear in your own home." She paused to take a breath, and Harvey burst out laughing.

"Wow, it's a good thing you stopped by. You doubled my sales with sixty seconds of awesome advice."

Nellie smiled sweetly. "Happy to help."

"And, really, we would be happy to help," I added.

Why was I always stammering around this man?

"If you need assistance with your display on Saturday, let us know. We can stop by that morning and add some ribbons, or whatever Nell suggests, to make sure shoppers fall in love with you. I mean, with your art. Your items." I shifted my gaze, pleading with my friend. "Right, Nellie?"

"Of course." She nodded calmly, pretending I hadn't just made a fool of myself. "May we take a peek at this piece you have hidden under the burlap?"

"Ah. I wondered when you would ask. This is an experiment. I could use an honest opinion." Removing the cloth, he turned to look at us anxiously.

"What do you think?"

We stared at the intricate wrought iron piece for several seconds before either of us spoke. I tilted my head to one side and looked at Nell from the corner of my eyes. "What do we think, Nell?"

"Could you hold it up for us?"

Carefully, he lifted the twenty-eight-inch piece by its center point, turning it into position. As he swiveled the fixture into place, the swirling lines of metal formed a reverse canopy with eight graceful candelabra holders reaching upward in an open scroll frame.

The words burst from my mouth in a sigh. "It's heavenly."

Then I stuck my foot in my mouth by continuing. "It looks like it's floating. It's so minimal I can't see where any cord would go. Does it work?"

"Josie," Nell cautioned.

I shrugged at her helplessly. "But it's made of this heavy metal, and it looks like it would break if someone blew on it."

Harvey clapped his hands and laughed out loud. "That's exactly what I was going for." He was so delighted that I couldn't help grinning along with him.

"It's an original design for a delicate chandelier to meld into a room, leaving the candelabra lights shining above. I hope someone will want to hang it in an entryway or over a big antique dining room table. And, yes, it does work. In fact, it can be fitted with standard electric candelabra bulbs or with dripless candles for a special occasion. Either way, it will light up the room."

"This is a masterpiece," Nellie said as she stepped back to admire the chandelier he held aloft. "I hope you will price this accordingly. And you must find a way to hang it for your display. Laying it on its side will not work."

"I'll do that," Harvey agreed. Lowering the chandelier, he glanced at his watch and then back toward the forge. "Was there any particular reason you ladies stopped by today other than to get a sneak peek at my Summer's End pieces?"

"I wanted to thank you again for helping me yesterday when I told you about Mr. Hamilton. And to tell you the whole town is now talking about his death, so there's no reason for you to keep it quiet."

"And here I thought we shared an important secret." He cocked his head at me, and I felt a rush of heat flow from my neck upward to flood my face. "But there really aren't any secrets in a town this size, right?"

I backed a few steps farther away, hoping he wouldn't notice my blush. "I guess you're right. Except, maybe, the name of the murderer. Nell and I are going to see the chief right now to tell him all the suspects we discovered when we met with Betty. I hope the guilty one is from out of town."

Harvey stacked several bars of iron next to his anvil before he answered. "Makes sense. No one wants to think they live next door to a killer."

Nellie stretched her hand out to Harvey. "It was so nice to see you again, Harvey. Let us know if you want help with your display. We have a group of mahjong ladies who would be happy to furnish cookbooks or other accessory items. Maybe Sharon would provide a fresh peach pie to set near the cookbook rack."

Harvey was still shaking his head and grinning as he waved to us from the doorway of the shop while we backed out of the parking spot.

I turned to my friend, noticing her crisp pressed shirt, and silver necklace and earrings. Never a hair out of place. "You are a wonder, Nellie. You have more decorating and display ideas in your head right now than I ever will."

"You are the wonder, Jo." Nell patted my hand, her eyes twinkling. "You still haven't realized that Harvey is interested in you."

"What? That's ridiculous, Nell. I'm old enough to be his...well, his much older sister."

"He's older than he looks." She frowned at me. "And you're certainly young enough to think about dating again. Keep an open mind."

I was still rolling my eyes over that when we arrived at the chief's office. "Let's forget about matchmaking and focus on murder-solving, shall we?"

But Nellie rolled her eyes right back at me.

Chapter Seven

Nellie and I arrived at the police station early, taking seats in a row of green metal chairs where we could see out the front window. We waited for several minutes, watching people as they stopped to report stolen bikes and sidewalk vandalism. Our little village wasn't accustomed to crime on a large scale.

I couldn't help thinking about how lucky I was to have Nellie by my side for this visit. She was smart and logical. I knew the chief would listen closely when Nellie talked. It didn't hurt that she'd lived in English Village far longer than I had. She knew about everybody—and their parents. She also had what I called "presence." When Nellie walked into a room, people automatically respected her. She walked and spoke with the confidence of a woman who had been raised to voice her opinion.

We perused the framed portraits of previous police chiefs along the front wall of the reception area. All of them had one thing in common: they were male. I knew the chief had tried to recruit more women into the department, but our small town was still behind the curve in that regard. Chief Marshall stepped into the entry promptly at 2:00 p.m. He wasted no time leading us down the hall.

"You ladies claim to have a list of suspects, and I'd like to know who they are," he said over his shoulder. "I've asked officer Devon to sit in on this meeting so he can take a few notes."

Ugh. Devon was a youngish patrolman. I guessed him to be around thirty-five, about the age of my younger son, but without an ounce of sense. We'd met before under different circumstances. He was the officer who found me breaking into my grandmother's cottage the day I arrived in town. A neighbor reported suspicious activity, and he rushed to the scene.

There I was, halfway through the bedroom window, with a puppy under one arm and my purse strap over the other. I had almost eased my stomach over the windowsill when I heard a shout behind me. "Police! Halt!"

Stunned at his command, I glanced over my shoulder, but the movement sent me off-balance, and gravity propelled me forward into an awkward pile on the bedroom floor. By the time I untangled my purse from the puppy and peered out the window, Officer Devon had drawn his weapon. It took me twenty minutes to convince him I owned the cottage.

Staring into the barrel of his gun, I raised my hands. "Do I look like a robber?"

The officer studied my smudged face and graying hair. He held steady and called for backup, his voice an octave higher. "Why did you go through the window?"

"Because the key broke in the lock, and I needed to get inside." I smiled to show him what a nice person I could be.

I could hear the siren of another squad car drawing nearer. Reading his badge, I tried to reason with him.

"Look, Officer Devon, if I wanted to rob the place, I wouldn't have towed a U-Haul into the driveway."

"Maybe you planned to carry out the furnishings," he proposed.

"What about my dog? You think I would have carried a puppy with me for a break and entry?"

The officer had no sense of humor. He shrugged.

After two additional patrolmen arrived, the officer finally holstered his gun. They all entered through the back door and helped me extricate the broken key from the lock. I showed them my deed to the cottage. Problem solved.

My opinion of Devon was influenced by that experience. I knew he listened carefully and paid attention to details. But I also felt he was too quick to jump to conclusions. I was glad he reported to Chief Marshall; the younger officer needed the balanced leadership the chief provided. Chief might be gruff at times, but he knew his stuff. Nonetheless, I wasn't excited about sharing our list with Devon in the room.

The chief ushered us into the small interview room that doubled as a conference room for the station. Devon rose from his seat as we entered.

Impressive. Did the chief signal him to stand?

Nellie tilted her head to acknowledge the gesture.

I took one look at the weathered old metal table, and my mind pictured dozens of suspects who might have been interrogated here. In the corner sat a glass coffee pot with a sliver of brown liquid scorched on the bottom. I wondered how long it had been sitting unattended. The chief saw my glance and nodded back at me. "That's not a drink I would offer a friend. Probably time to make a fresh pot."

He and Devon sat on one side of the table; Nellie and I took seats across from them. Suddenly, the serious nature of this visit hit me hard. I hesitated, afraid we shouldn't provide the names we had selected after all. What did we really know about them, anyway? I gave Nellie a panicked look.

Again, the chief seemed to read my mind. He looked deeply into my worried face and gave me a reassuring smile. "It's okay, Josie. This is simply a conversation. You're not accusing anyone of murder. You are only here to help me identify some folks who may have a relationship with Betty or Bob that I wouldn't know about. Perhaps they will be able to provide more information that leads to the murderer."

His calm, comforting manner set my mind at ease. I thought about what a good man he was. His little girl, Suzy, was one of the dancers at Miss Betty's School of Dance. The chief wanted to solve this murder like we did, and for some of the same reasons.

So, Nellie and I went through our list. We told the chief how we heard about each person and why we put each one on the list. He asked us questions, and we tried our best to give him good answers. Nellie announced each name like she was calling attendance in an elementary school classroom—which she did as a teacher for nearly fifteen years before she went to work helping her husband, Tim, with his growing furniture store business.

"Michael Wilson." She declared the name with precision. "He's in love with

Betty and has been since they met in college. They have a lot in common. They were both former dancers in NYC. They both like flowers; he's a botanist, and she has beautiful flower gardens surrounding her house. And he sends her flowers every week."

The chief nodded. "I understand the two were introduced by a mutual friend who served in the Marine Corps with Bob."

We stared at him, surprised.

He raised an eyebrow. "I have a few sources of my own. Who's next?"

Nellie announced suspect number two. "Thomas Fisher. He's the marine who introduced Bob to Betty. She told us Michael never forgave him for making the introduction. He's in town this week for a visit. Apparently, Thomas also hoped to date Betty at one time. She must have been an attractive young woman in her twenties."

I turned to face the chief. "She's beautiful now. With that fabulous platinum hair and Elizabeth Taylor eyes."

"I'll give you that," the chief said. "She's a lovely woman. More importantly, she seems to be a genuinely nice person. I will talk to Sergeant. Fisher."

"Our friend Kate was in the Marine Corps, too. She says there's no way a marine would use poison to kill anyone. A real marine would use a gun or his bare hands."

The chief laughed so loud I thought he was going to burst his buttons. "Is that right, Josie? He wouldn't consider using another weapon, even to throw someone off the track? I appreciate Kate's support of her fellow marine, but I'll make my own judgment about his innocence, if you don't mind."

"Of course." I folded my hands primly on the table. "I wanted you to know everything we considered."

"As you should. Who's next on your list, Nell?"

"Alyssa Burney," Nell said without hesitation and pointed to the girl's name. "She's the young ballet apprentice who helps Betty at the studio."

The chief tapped his pen on the table. "I know her. She teaches my daughter Suzy's class. But she doesn't seem like a murderer to me."

"We put her on the list because Betty mentioned Alyssa is quite ambitious for a twenty-two-year-old. Plus, she's always bringing Bob special treats when she comes by the house. She baked him homemade brownies and other favorites. She had the opportunity to poison him."

The chief nodded and rubbed his chin. "I don't know what her motive would be. What would she gain with Bob gone?" He thought for a moment and made a note on the pad in front of him.

"Anyone else?"

"Two more. Nellie?"

"Pete Scott." She pronounced the name with a flourish. "He's a gardener who uses part of the Hamilton land to grow his produce for the village market. We added him because he gives the Hamiltons lots of free produce in return for the use of their land. He could have poisoned Bob."

"Possibly. Who else have you got?"

"Larry Fox," Nell announced dramatically.

"The dog walker?" The chief shook his head. "He's an odd duck, but I don't think he fits the profile of a murderer."

I made an X beside the young man's name. "Probably not. He's on our list because Betty said he and Bob argued recently. She wasn't sure what it was about, but Bob was upset. He didn't want Larry to walk their Labradoodle, Tinkerbelle."

Nellie chimed in by waving her notes in the air. "Our friend Sharon told us Barbara Chamberlin said Larry sometimes hangs out in front of the ballet studio. You know, Barbara owns the Pet Stop next door to Miss Betty's. She thinks Larry might be sweet on Betty."

The chief raised an eyebrow. "Well, if you say that Sharon said that Barbara told her Larry has a crush on Betty, it must be true."

Officer Devon snorted in the corner.

"Are you doubting our sources?" I sat taller in my seat.

Chief Marshall stifled a smile and shifted his gaze between Nellie and me. "Not at all. I'm trying to get the sequence straight in my mind."

"OK, then." Nellie exhaled.

The chief turned to Devon. "Anything you want to ask?"

"No, sir. I think I've got it."

"Well then, let's let these ladies get back to their day. I trust the two of you

43

have other things to do?"

"We sure do." Nell waved another list at the chief. "The Summer's End Festival is two days away. We've got plenty to keep us busy. The village will be filled with tourists."

I watched as the chief shook Nell's hand and thanked her for coming in. Then, he turned to me. "Josie, you know I appreciate your help. But I want you to step away now and let me do my job."

"Yes, Chief," I promised. And I meant it when I said it. But that was before I got the call from Kate, and we decided to take our dogs to the park. How was I to know we would run right into Larry Fox himself?

Chapter Eight

Kate and I often walked together to the park so our dogs could play. Her rescued Goldendoodle, Bacon, was almost as big as my Old English sheepdog, Moe. Both were sturdy good-natured dogs with plenty of fluffy curls. The two had been buddies since shortly after I'd moved into the village. We were delighted to discover we had adopted them within a couple of weeks of each other. This "park time" was good for the dogs, but I'll admit it was also good for their owners. It was the only time Kate and I had to visit, and we enjoyed sharing all the latest village gossip.

Every time I saw Kate, I was reminded of Dorothy from *The Golden Girls*. Not because she looked like any of the actors—because she didn't, really—although she had lovely short silver hair. But more because Dorothy and Kate were both quick-witted, and a bit sarcastic, when necessary. I remembered one episode of the long-running TV show where Dorothy stood up and practically shouted at the friends gathered around her: "What? Are you telling me I am the only one who enjoys diagramming sentences?" I had no doubt that Kate might have made the same proclamation on occasion. She loved structure, and she was the first to remind us of the rules when we played our weekly mahjong games.

Despite all of her witty comments, Kate never wanted to hurt anyone's feelings. She hid a sensitive side behind the sarcasm. She was both funny and caring. The two of us were the only widowed members of our circle of friends. We enjoyed every minute with the Mahjong Mavens, but sometimes it was fun to visit separately with another single woman.

Except for me, the mavens were all in their mid-sixties, so they had plenty of stories to tell. I loved listening to news about Kate's kids and grandkids, and she returned the favor when I had news about my sons. Tonight, we walked at a leisurely pace and stopped to sit awhile on the little bench beside the Hank English statue. Suddenly, we heard a commotion that sounded like a cacophony of barking dogs chasing a squirrel. Bacon and Moe strained on their leashes as Kate and I struggled to keep them contained at our sides.

Soon, we saw the source of the noisy racket. Larry Fox rounded the corner with three little terriers who had tangled their leashes and were struggling to free themselves. The agile dog walker expertly raised the leashes over his head, did a quick pirouette beneath them, and separated the three with ease. I have to say it was impressive. Kate and I burst out laughing, and Larry sheepishly walked the dogs a little closer to our bench.

"I'm sorry you ladies had to see that." The twenty-six-year-old stood in front of us to apologize, his three terriers now docile at his feet. The dog walker was slender, with longish hair that now stuck out in unruly wisps all over his head. "I pride myself on being able to control these puppies, but tonight they got the best of me when a stray rabbit popped out of those bushes along the sidewalk."

We grinned back at him. Kate motioned to the pups as they gathered round the doggy water fountain, noisily lapping from the full basin. "Looks like they're ready to take a break."

The young man gave a sidelong glance toward the thirsty terriers. "I'm working the night shift at my regular job tonight, so I wanted to exercise them before I returned them to their owner."

I looked up at the dog walker from my seat on the park bench. "I didn't realize you worked two jobs."

"Yeah. I'm paying off student loans. I work nights at the Curiosity Shop, helping Mr. McGregor restock shelves and clean up a bit. You'd be surprised how many clocks we wind and dust every night."

Kate cleared her throat and looked up at the young man. "How's the dog-walking business so far? You've always been good with my sweet Bacon, but I heard that you had a run-in with Betty's husband about their dog last week."

I gasped and glared at Kate. "You can't ask a guy about an unhappy customer. He might not want to talk about it."

Kate was unflappable. "If you want to know something, you have to ask."

I turned to Larry and rolled my eyes.

The dog walker shrugged. "It wasn't a big deal. Mr. Hamilton was screaming at his dog Tinkerbelle about eating Betty's flowers. He hit her with a stick, and I yelled at him to stop. I never understood why someone would punish a dog for doing what comes naturally to them. What's a bunch of flowers compared to the loyalty of man's best friend? We got into a shouting match, and I walked away."

Kate ducked her head. "Sorry, I didn't mean to pry. I was curious."

"Well, I'm glad you made him think about his actions," I added as I pulled Moe closer to distance him from the three smaller terriers. "I probably would have done the same thing,"

Larry's herd of puppies strained against their leashes. "I better get back to it," he said, following the terriers back toward the sidewalk, and I nudged Kate. "Nice job. Now we know what the argument was about."

She flashed me her famous "told-you-so" grin. "I figured the direct approach might be our best opportunity to gather some information."

We walked farther through the park to the fork where we would each head toward our separate homes. Kate turned to me. "I almost forgot to tell you what Sharon saw at pickleball today. Bob's marine buddy, Thomas Fisher, showed up to play and got into a huge argument with Betty's former dance partner."

"Michael Wilson? Betty didn't mention he was in town."

"That's the one. Sharon was really surprised. Neither of them is a regular at the pickleball court, so it was odd for both to appear on the same day. Then, out of nowhere, they were yelling at each other. Another player had to separate them and send them both out the door."

"Hmm. I'd like to know what started the argument and what he is doing here," I said. "Maybe you should ask them. That's what I would do."

"I'm sure you would," I said. "But I promised the chief I would stay out of this."

Kate snorted. "That's not going to happen. You'll be up all night until you figure it out."

By the time Moe and I walked home, I was ready to shove all the murder suspects out of my mind and put my feet up. I fed Moe and made myself a sandwich. Before I bit into it, my cell phone rang.

"Hi, Sharon," I said after recognizing her number.

"I'm so glad you picked up," she said breathlessly. "I have news to share, and it might be important."

"What happened?"

Sharon began by explaining she had been out running errands and arrived back at her house to find Betty standing on her front porch. "She was returning my pie pan. And of course, I told her that wasn't necessary. She must have so many other details to take care of, with Bob's funeral and everything."

I kept listening. I knew Sharon would tell me the news in her own time.

"Have you really looked into Betty's eyes? They aren't blue. They're violet. Absolutely gorgeous. With those eyes and that halo of platinum hair, she is striking. "

"Yes. She's lovely." Sharon sighed before she continued.

"Oh, sorry. I got off track. We talked about cooking. And, the thing is, she never cooked."

"Never?"

"Never. Bob did it all. The grocery shopping. The meals. The snacks. He controlled the kitchen just as he controlled her life."

"Then how could she have poisoned him?"

I heard the glee in Sharon's voice. "She couldn't. Betty had no way to poison her husband's food, even if she wanted to."

"But, if Betty didn't kill him, who did? And how did they administer the poison?" I asked.

"That's what you have to figure out, Josie."

I thanked Sharon for the call and added another note card to my stack: Betty. Never. Cooked. As I lifted my sandwich to my lips, my cell rang again. I answered with a laugh. "Hey, Sharon, did you think of something else?"

But it wasn't Sharon on the other end. At first, I heard only heavy breathing.

Then, the line went dead. I looked into my sweet dog's brown eyes. "What do you think about that, Moe? Somebody had the wrong number."

Before anything else could interrupt me, I set the phone aside and grabbed my sandwich. Tomorrow would be our last day to prepare for the Summer's End Festival, and it would be a busy one.

Chapter Nine

Friday morning, I woke early. I couldn't get the conversation with the dog walker out of my mind. Something didn't add up. I wondered about his story of Bob punishing Tinkerbelle for getting into Betty's flowers. He doted on that dog. Without really thinking, I called Betty to verify the story. She answered immediately.

"I'm sorry to call so early," I apologized after identifying myself, "but I ran into Larry Fox at the park yesterday afternoon, and he told me a story about a disagreement he had with Bob. I remembered that you mentioned an argument, too."

Betty thought for a moment before she answered. "Larry is basically a nice guy. Bob and I spoke to him a few times about helping out with Tinkerbelle, but we never actually hired him."

"Can you tell me why?" I dared to ask.

"It's a little more complicated . . . than the disagreement. But I don't think it was serious enough to lead to murder."

"Did Bob really lose his temper when Tinkerbelle trampled your flowers? Hit her with a stick?"

"Oh, no. Bob would never strike Tinkerbelle. It's true that he yelled at her for digging in the flower bed. They're my favorite flower, and Bob planted them all around our property. He watched over them because he knew how much I enjoyed them. They're a garden flower, not really meant for commercial flower arrangements. So, they were a special flower no one else could send me."

I thought about the hidden meaning behind Betty's story. While Bob was aware that Betty's friend Michael often sent her flowers, this variety was one only Bob could share with his wife.

"Bob always said they were free-spirited flowers, like me. Privately, he sometimes called me his *belladonna*. Pretty woman. It always made me smile because *Amaryllis belladonna* is the Latin name for the Naked Lady."

"I've been wondering about them. Do they bloom all year?"

"No. That's another thing that makes them special. They only bloom in late July or early August, depending on the weather. Bob was so determined to have the blossoms all year that he built the greenhouse simply to grow Naked Ladies."

"He really cared about those flowers," I said as I jotted another note on the pad beside me.

Betty sighed. "To him, anyone who harmed the flowers harmed me. But there was another, more important reason that he was upset with Tinkerbelle. Bob knew the Naked Lady blooms were toxic to dogs. He didn't want Tinkerbelle to make herself sick eating the blossoms. He explained that to Larry, but the dog walker wouldn't listen."

Hearing the full story, I realized it couldn't have been easy for Bob to share his beautiful wife with her friend Michael. He believed Betty when she said she had no romantic feelings toward the botanist, but he also knew Michael was deeply in love with Betty. No wonder Bob wanted to keep this one flower as something special between himself and his wife.

"Beyond the incident with the flowers," Betty continued, "Bob simply didn't care for Larry. The dog walker often showed up at the ballet studio right before closing. After class ended, he sometimes came inside to ask if we needed any help closing. He offered to take out our trash—that kind of thing."

"Was he trying to get closer to you?"

"Bob thought he had a crush on me. I never agreed. Larry and I rarely spoke."

"So, he never tried to approach you or flirt with you?"

"Heavens, no. I think he was a little lonely. I didn't sense that he had any interest in the ballet—or in me. But Bob didn't want to encourage him to hang around. So, we never hired him to walk Tinkerbelle."

I thanked her for indulging my questions, tucking the new information into the back of my mind. She was probably right. Larry was a young man who liked dogs and was trying to get his business going. He appeared to be a hard worker taking on extra jobs to make ends meet.

While I felt better about crossing Larry off my suspect list, I still had a nagging thought about Betty's former dance partner, Michael. I couldn't help thinking it was important for the chief to know about the incident on the pickleball court. Sighing, I made the call to Chief Marshall. Luckily, it went straight through to voicemail, so I wouldn't have to listen to his admonitions that I stay out of his investigation. Instead, I left a brief message:

"Chief, you probably already know, but Michael Wilson and Thomas Fisher got into a big kerfuffle at pickleball yesterday afternoon. It might be nothing, but I thought you would want to check it out."

Then I remembered my conversation with Sharon, so I called the chief again and waited for the beep. "Plus, Sharon said that Betty said she never cooks. Bob makes his own meals." I hung up without leaving my name. I'm pretty sure the chief had my number on his speed dial by now. He would know the messages were from me.

Moe stared at me with his head cocked to the side like he always did when he wanted my attention. I leaned down to scratch his belly and assured him that I was almost ready to leave the house. That silly dog knew me better than anyone, though. He scrambled to his feet and moseyed over to the basket next to our front door. Picking up his leash, he dragged it to my side and placed it on my lap.

"Well, aren't you the smart one." I gave him another scratch behind his ears. "Yes, we're going out. Give me five minutes more to put on my shoes."

I made good on my promise to Moe, but we completed our walk in record time. I was happy to have finished a full circle around the park while the air was still a cool 80 degrees. By the time we returned, I had decided to do as the chief asked — let him handle the murder investigation without my help. It was his job to protect our little village, and I knew he took it seriously. Moe and I were barely back inside the cottage when my phone rang. Thinking it would be Nellie doing her daily check-in, I pulled the phone from my purse and answered playfully, "Yes, Mom, I'm up and dressed."

Harvey's big laugh on the other end of the line took me by surprise. "Er, sorry," I said, thankful he couldn't see my deep blush of embarrassment. "I thought you were Nellie. She calls about this time every day to see what I have planned."

"Good to know someone is checking on you." I could hear the chuckle in his voice.

"It is. I try to tell her I can take care of myself, but she still gives me a quick call to check in. She's a good friend."

"Actually, I was calling to ask you about Nellie."

For a quick moment, I felt a twinge of…disappointment?

"Do you need her phone number?" I asked.

"No, I hoped you could tell me whether the two of you were serious about helping with my booth for Summer's End? I have been working so hard to finish the pieces that I didn't think about how to display them until you stopped by yesterday. The show is tomorrow, and all I have is the table you saw at the shop."

I knew without asking that all the Mahjong Mavens would be happy to help if they could.

"Relax, Harvey. We will have your display ready and waiting for you bright and early tomorrow morning."

Then I hung up the phone and realized one important fact: We had less than twenty-four hours to assemble a booth we hadn't designed yet.

Chapter Ten

Half an hour later, the Mahjong Mavens were assembled at The Cozy Cups. Today, I noticed a smattering of out-of-towners who were probably here to set up booths for the festival.

As usual, we claimed the "conversation corner" and settled ourselves onto the couch and chairs while Lorene Marshall, the chief's wife, took our orders. The Mahjong Mavens loved Lorene. She was a strong businesswoman with a passion for customer service. I once saw Lorene go toe-to-toe with a trucker who thought he could disrespect one of her young servers. She rose to her full four-foot-ten height and shook her finger in the big guy's face. Her hand barely reached above his elbows, but he got the message. I almost laughed out loud. The trucker took the scolding like it had come from his grandmother instead a diminutive Asian lady. He apologized profusely and left the young waitress a fat tip.

Before we tackled the challenge of planning Harvey's booth, Sharon pulled me aside. "I have to ask you a personal question."

"What is it?"

"Nellie told me her brother-in-law, Jimmy, played basketball with Harvey in high school."

"Yes?"

"Well, my little brother was on the same team. And, well, they all hung out together." Suddenly, I knew where this conversation was going. "That's what I heard."

"They really liked Harvey back then. They still do. They haven't been as close, because he left to go to college and didn't come back to English Village until recently."

"He's a nice man," I said neutrally.

"Yes. Well, my question is, do you like him?

"Of course, I like him."

"No, I mean, do you really like him? Because if you do, we could arrange to get the two of you together." She paused and stared at me. "For a date."

I sighed. "Sharon, while I do like Harvey. I haven't considered dating anyone since my husband died. Besides, I can't imagine Harvey having any interest in me. I'm quite a bit older than he is, don't you think?"

"There's not that much difference between you,"

Sharon scoffed. "He's my brother's age—so fifty-ish. You're barely fifty-five. What are five or six years?"

"Look, I appreciate you thinking about me, but I don't know very much about him. We probably don't have anything in common."

"Yes, you do. He's been single for thirteen years. He has a daughter in college. You have two adult sons. You both like living in our little village. What more do you need to know?"

I laughed at her enthusiasm. "How about if we let things move at their own pace? Harvey is a new friend. He's a bit younger than I am. And, while I like talking to him, I'm definitely not ready to ask him for a date."

"Are you sure you don't want me to arrange something?"

"Please don't."

She glanced across the table toward Nellie and shrugged her shoulders, giving her a small shake of her head. "I told you so," Nellie mouthed back.

Thankfully, the subject was soon forgotten. We all chattered away with ideas for Harvey's booth. Nellie announced she and Sharon had already talked to their husbands about building a frame for Harvey's display. She unrolled a large poster and spread it on the table. "We made a diagram."

"The guys are taking that old wood Tim had stored in our garage. They are building two display walls, with connecting crossbeams and a latticework back side." Nellie pointed to each section as she described the plans. "It won't take them more than a couple of hours to do, and we will have plenty of hooks and shelves to display Harvey's wares."

Sharon nodded, then added, "That sounds perfect. I'll take care of displaying his cookbook holders and pie racks. I'm writing recipe cards, and I'll bring an assortment of cookbooks to set into the racks. If there's room, we can set a pie beside them. Are there any other kitchen items to go in this section?"

I glanced down at the list of products from my notes. "He has some dishcloth holders. It would be good to have towels in a couple of those."

"I've got that covered, too," Sharon noted from across the table. "And I'll bring some snacks tonight when we meet to put it all together."

Nellie pointed to the diagram of the lattice wall planned for the back of the booth. "I have plenty of candles for those sconces he made. We could hang them here…and here. And I'll pick up some fresh flowers to go into the wall vases."

"Let me get the flowers," I said. "I need to go by the Garden Cart this afternoon for another potted plant anyway."

"Josie and I will also make price tags and a poster for the front of the booth," Kate volunteered for the two of us. I indicated my approval with a thumbs-up.

From her experience in the military, Kate was always prepared for anything. She looked at Nell. "I will also bring a calculator and some change. I have one of those cell phone credit card gadgets if Harvey wants to borrow and connect it to his bank account. That way, people can pay with a credit card if they want."

Sharon clapped her hands. "What a great idea. Can we use that for the garage sale later this fall? I'm already filling boxes."

Kate shrugged. "Sure. It's simple, and more dependable than taking a check from a stranger."

"Ladies, don't forget you can always get rid of your old trinkets and treasures by putting them out on The Corner," Nellie announced. "They never fail to disappear."

I must have looked puzzled because Nellie leaned over to whisper an explanation. "The Corner is a spot near the alley behind Tim's cabinetry store. About once a month, Tim sets old scraps into a pile on The Corner, and the next day they are gone."

Everyone laughed at Nell's suggestion. I grinned back at her. "Well, I certainly hope we won't be putting Harvey's leftover items out there. I'll be surprised if they aren't all sold by mid-afternoon."

With everything covered, we agreed to gather our decorating items and meet Harvey at the blacksmith shop at seven that evening. Together, we would make sure everything fit and prepare a final checklist for Saturday morning. It wouldn't take long to set up the booth once the display panels were in place.

I threw my purse over my shoulder and pulled my sunglasses from their perch on the top of my head. The summer sun was blazing hot again, and I couldn't wait to get back home to work on Harvey's display poster. The other ladies were right behind me as I stepped out from under the café's awning and walked right into Chief Marshall.

He stopped in front of me, blocking the sidewalk. "You're the one I wanted to see."

"I came to tell you—and all your posse—that your friend's tip turned out to be a dead end."

The chief drew us closer as though he was a coach, and we were his teammates. "Here's the latest: Remember the kerfuffle between the marine and the botanist?"

Four heads nodded in unison.

"I checked it out, and I'm convinced it had nothing to do with the murder."

Four women sighed as one. "Aww."

"These two men apparently behave like high school rivals every time they see each other. Thomas Fisher, the marine, and Michael Wilson, the botanist, have an old grudge related to the botanist's undying love for Betty. The marine is the one who introduced her to Bob. Now every time they see each other, the botanist blasts the marine for taking Betty away from him. This argument simmers until they see each other again—which happens rarely—and then it erupts into the same scenario. It's one of those feuds that will never die."

"You don't believe either of them is the murderer?" I asked.

"No, Josie, I interviewed each of them individually and checked their alibis."

Frankly, I was a little disappointed, and I knew Sharon felt the same. That pickleball argument seemed like a solid clue. The chief encouraged us to forget about murder investigations and enjoy the Summer's End festivities. "I'll take it from here," he said as he waved goodbye and walked toward the police station.

Standing on the sidewalk, I thought I saw a flicker of movement across the street in the doorway of Miss Betty's School of Dance as if someone was spying on us, but it was gone when I looked again. The other three decided to head home. We had too much to do to be dawdling here in the sun.

Before I returned to my cottage, I crossed the street to visit The Pet Stop next door to Miss Betty's. I couldn't resist the sign in the window: CHEESY PLEASY SCONES FOR HAPPY PUPS. I stepped inside the shop and headed directly for the display counter. The home-baked treats were Moe's favorite, and they were only available when the shop's owner had time to make them. Inside, The Pet Stop smelled like bacon and butter, and my mouth watered. Barb walked through the swinging door from her kitchen.

Barbara Chamberlin was another of the local women who decided to spend her retirement years in a second career here. She was a lifelong resident of English Village; in fact, her grandfather was one of the town's founders. Barbara had spent most of her adult life working for nonprofits, but she also had a soft spot for animals. Now, she devoted her time to discovering special gifts and treats pet owners couldn't resist. I had quickly become one of her best customers.

"You've been baking again," I called to her from across the display case.

Barbara greeted me with a smile. "Welcome back, Josie." Her short dark hair was styled into a pixie cut that gave her a youthful look. Today she wore a bright red apron over her traditional black pants and top. In bold letters, the apron read: **PET STOP TREATS ARE DOGGONE GOOD.**

I pointed to the golden treats on the top shelf. "I'm here for the *Cheesy Pleasy* scones. Moe can't get enough of them."

Barbara laughed. "I saw you out front and already bagged a half-dozen for you. My treat. You've referred so many customers, it's the least I can do."

"Oh, no. I'm happy to pay for them." I took my wallet from my handbag and handed her twenty dollars.

"That works for me." She accepted the money without argument and counted out my change. "But I'm adding a couple of my new Sticky Paws Peanut Butter biscuits for him to try. That's what I will be promoting for my Summer's End booth tomorrow. Let me know if Moe approves them. His endorsement is my best advertisement."

I headed back out to my car, smiling. I almost forgot that a murderer was at loose in our village.

Chapter Eleven

I hadn't walked ten steps outside the Pet Stop before a little warning bell went off in my head. Well, it wasn't a bell, exactly. It was that nagging feeling that I'd forgotten something. I turned around and walked back to Miss Betty's School of Dance next door. The studio was closed, but my mind wouldn't rest until I checked to see if anyone was inside.

I glanced over my shoulder at our little Main Street shops. Everything seemed in order. People walked in and out of Cozy Cups. Mr. Nutter pulled his food truck into the lot at the end of the block. Two young boys rode their bicycles toward the library. I reached the studio door and cupped my hands around my eyes to peer inside the glass. The lights were off, and the hallway was deserted.

To be certain, I took my keys from my purse and used them to make a louder noise as I knocked sharply on the frame of the door. I counted to thirty and knocked again. Then, just as I decided I was being silly, I saw it. There was a shadow reflected by the light bouncing off the floor-to-ceiling mirrors in the studio. Suddenly, a slim silhouette appeared at the end of the hallway and walked directly toward me.

I smiled at Alyssa as she unlocked the door, opening it wide for me to enter. "Is something wrong?" Her brow wrinkled in concern.

"That was going to be my question for you. I thought I saw someone moving around in the studio, and I knew it couldn't be Betty."

Alyssa smiled back at me with wide, innocent eyes. She switched on the lights. "No, everything is fine here. Betty asked me to pick up a few things the girls will need for their performance tomorrow."

"Are you still doing a show at the gazebo?"

"Yes. The little ballerinas have worked too hard to cancel it. Their parents have invited their grandparents, and everyone is excited to see them dance."

"Will you be here at the studio much longer? I could wait for you." The surrounding dark hallways and mirrored walls gave me a spooky vibe.

Alyssa shook her head. "No, I'm fine." She picked up a bright pink dance bag and slung it over her shoulder. "I have a key, and it's not unusual for me to come in after hours or on the weekends. Betty even lets me study here when I need a quiet place."

I peered around the deserted studio and looked back at the young dancer. "It sounds like you're all set. I'm sorry to have interrupted you."

"That's okay." Alyssa stepped closer to where I stood near the door. "Are you making any progress on solving Bob's murder?"

I shook my head, startled she would presume I was involved. "Of course not. That's the chief's job."

"You and your mahjong ladies aren't asking questions around town?" Alyssa now stood directly in front of me. "Betty seems to think you are going to find the murderer."

"We have some ideas, but we're turning our leads over to the chief."

"Do you think you know who did it?" She looked at me, her wide eyes unwavering.

"Let's say we're getting closer."

"Well, let me know if I can help." Tears filled the girl's eyes. "I really liked Mr. Hamilton. And I would do anything for Betty."

For a fraction of a second, that little bell rang in my head again. Then, I gave the girl a hug and told her not to worry.

Leaving Alyssa to lock up the ballet studio, I made the short walk home. My little cottage was cool inside, and Moe welcomed me with a wag that shook his entire body. I gave him one of Barbara's *Cheesy Pleasy* scones before I let him out to play in the fenced backyard. Then I gathered the poster materials for Harvey's display booth.

It didn't take long to spread an eight-foot stretch of banner-weight vinyl along the floor beneath my living room's bay window. I stacked books on each end to hold the fabric in place. Then, I sketched the letters lightly in pencil, spacing them evenly across the banner. I stood to survey the message:

HARVEY'S HANDCRAFTED METAL ARTWORKS

The text was a little off-center, but it would be fine from a distance. Now all I had to do was fill in the lettering with paint and figure out how to keep Moe from adding his paw prints to the wet banner. I peeked out the window to see Moe stretched out in the shade of a huge walnut tree that graced the corner of our garden. He seemed content, but I knew he would be ready to come in as soon as I dared to start applying color to the banner.

After pondering my options for a few minutes, I pulled the dog walker's business card from the top drawer of my desk. He answered in a friendly, professional voice so perfectly rehearsed I thought it might be a recording.

"Thanks for calling Larry the Dog Walker."

"Larry, it's Josie."

"Hi, Josie." He hesitated a fraction too long before he continued. "Is something wrong?"

For a moment, I wondered why he would ask the same question I had heard from Alyssa. But then I realized I had never called him to walk Moe before.

"No, everything's fine. I wondered if you might have time to come walk Moe. I have a painting project I need to do at the house, and I can't have him traipsing over it."

"Sure. I'm open in an hour if that works for you."

"He's already had one walk today, so he won't want to go far. I need someone to take him away from here for at least forty-five minutes."

Larry laughed. "I get it. I can keep him occupied for an hour. We won't go far. Maybe I could let him explore the wooded area over by the art museum. It has huge shade trees and plenty of squirrels to chase. If there's time, we can go to the new dog park."

"That sounds perfect. Moe gets to explore a new place, and I'll have time to complete my project."

I gave him my address and ended the call with a satisfied sigh. By the time Larry stopped by to get Moe, I had eaten lunch, showered, and slipped into a fresh pair of shorts. Harvey's product list was stenciled onto a poster-size art card, and I was ready to fill in the lettering with bright colors.

Larry presented a release form for me to sign before he accepted Moe's leash. "It's a formality, but I like to know I'm doing what you want."

I worked quickly through the form, filling in Moe's name, breed, veterinarian, and current shots. I checked that Moe was allowed to go off-leash in the local dog park, play in the water feature there, and accept dog biscuits as treats for good behavior. I completed the form with my signature, the date, and my cell number.

"Let's go, buddy." Larry whistled to Moe, and they headed down the sidewalk.

Moe looked back at me as if to say, "Hey, aren't you coming with us?" But I waved them on, and he happily trotted off beside his new friend.

Thirty minutes later, I sat with my feet propped on the ottoman, a glass of iced tea on the table beside me. I admired my work with a critical eye. The poster and banner lay side-by-side on the floor to dry. I wondered what Harvey would think about his booth when we shared the plans with him. The Mahjong Mavens could be a little overbearing, on occasion. In this case, I felt sure he would appreciate our efforts.

I glanced at my watch and saw that I had another twenty minutes before Larry would return with Moe. The luxury of time to myself was rare. With the murder still hovering in my mind, I carried my laptop into the living room and flipped it open. I planned to search for background information on our primary suspects; instead, I felt myself relaxing into the soft, oversized chair.

My thoughts strayed to the dog walker and his fledgling business. While I loved having an Old English sheepdog in a town named English Village, Moe was a high-maintenance dog. He needed daily walks, regular grooming, and plenty of social interaction. A weekly appointment with Larry might be worth the expense.

I must have dozed off because I woke to the insistent ringing of my cell phone. Groggy, I picked it up. "This is Josie."

The voice on the other end was low, so I couldn't decipher who it was. But

I understood the message clearly. "You and your mavens need to stop what you're doing."

Suddenly, I was awake and listening for clues. It was a male voice. Muffled, like there might be a cloth over the phone or even a phone app to disguise the tone. "Stop now, or somebody's going to get hurt."

"Who is this?" I asked, my voice shaking.

"You could be next."

The call went dead, and I punched in Chief Marshall's number. He heard the fear in my voice before I could tell him what had happened. "Jo, I want you to take a deep breath." The chief was calm and composed. "Inhale slowly, and count to ten as you exhale. Can you do that for me?"

I followed his instructions and immediately began to feel more in control. "Yes."

"Are you hurt?"

"No."

"Are you alone?"

"Yes."

"Lock your door. I'm on my way."

Seconds later, my doorbell rang.

My heart raced as I peeked out the window. It was Larry, returning with Moe. I tried to look normal as I opened the door, but my face must have told a different story.

"Are you all right, Ms. Posey? You look pale."

"I'm fine, Larry," I lied and took the leash.

Larry gazed around my living room, waiting.

"Thanks for taking Moe." I slipped some cash into his hand and promised to call him again soon.

Chief Marshall pulled into my drive before Larry was off the porch. He nodded at him as he stepped into the house.

Chief scowled at me. "I thought I told you to lock the door."

"I did. I only let Larry come in to deliver Moe."

"You do realize he is still on our suspect list?" The chief raised an eyebrow and gave me a look I won't forget soon.

"Oh, yeah," I answered meekly, my knees wobbly.

The chief took my arm gently and led me to the kitchen table. "Sit. Now tell me exactly what happened."

I told him about the phone call, and he listened, nodding. "Now, tell me again. Start earlier in the day. What did you do today? Who did you see? Where did you go?"

Again, the chief listened as I described my day: a call to Betty (he frowned), meeting the mavens at Cozy Cups, stopping at the pet bakery, knocking on the door at the dance studio (another frown), making the poster, calling Larry to take Moe. He made me fill in the blanks to complete a timeline in his mind. I explained that I also ate a snack, took a shower, and dozed off in my chair.

"Repeat the part about the phone call. Tell me the exact words of the call and anything you remember about the caller's voice." I recited every detail as the chief jotted notes.

When he was certain I had told him everything, the chief placed his notepad on the table and looked directly into my eyes. "You've touched a nerve with someone. Here's what we're going to do." He raised his index finger to emphasize his point. "First, you will keep your door locked at all times until further notice."

"Yes," I nodded. I had never been so willing to follow instructions.

The chief held up two fingers. "Next, you will not leave the house without an escort."

"But, I have Moe," I argued weakly.

"Josie, this is important. Moe's a good dog, but he can't keep you safe. The presence of another person beside you will deter many bad guys from taking any action."

"Okay, I can ask a friend to go with me whenever I'm out."

The chief nodded his agreement. Then he held up three fingers. "Third, I want you to agree to a signal that will tell me you are safely at home."

"How would I do that?"

We talked about options and decided to keep it simple. The chief assigned a patrol car to drive by my house every hour for the next couple of days. If my porch light was on, they would know everything was fine. If it was off, something was not right.

"If anything happens to disturb you, call me. But, if you're not able to call, find a way to switch the porch light off, and we will know to look into it."

"I really believe the call was someone's idea of a prank," I protested. Now that the chief was here in my living room, I began to doubt my earlier reaction. "This seems like too much to ask of you."

Chief Marshall sighed and leaned against my kitchen island. "Please do as I say. It can't hurt. Plus, our little village is easy to drive. Patrolmen are going down your street all the time. This gives them a way to check on you without knocking on your door every hour."

Before leaving, the chief checked the locks on my windows and doors. We turned on the porch light. I set the deadbolt in place. And he drove away.

I never imagined I would need to use our private signal that very night.

Chapter Twelve

Nellie pulled into my drive promptly at six-thirty that evening. I carefully set the poster and the rolled banner into the trunk of her car, opened the back door for Moe to climb inside, and took my place in the passenger seat. On our way to the blacksmith shop, we drove to the Garden Cart to get fresh flowers for Harvey's display. My favorite local flower shop was a tiny little place run by Jill Pinkerton, the pastor's wife. She opened the shop shortly after they moved into English Village.

Nellie and Moe waited in the car while I ran inside. The heady scent of roses and gardenias filled the air, and I walked directly to the coolers where floral sprigs were displayed. Another customer stood at the cash register, his back toward the door. While Jill assisted him, I selected several bundles of lavender and heather.

I didn't intend to eavesdrop, but when Jill said, "We will deliver the basket to Mrs. Hamilton in the morning," my ears perked up. I edged a little closer to the counter and cast a sidelong glance at the man. I figured he was in his mid-thirties. Tall and handsome, with gentle eyes.

"Thank you for the special effort on this one," he said, handing her his credit card.

"It's our pleasure, Mr. Wilson. Did you want to include a card?"

"My usual." He slid a small white square of paper across the counter.

I listened closely to his voice, trying to determine whether he might have been my mystery caller.

With such a short conversation, it was impossible to discern. He saw me waiting and nodded politely in my direction as he left the shop. I stepped up to the counter.

My mind flooded with questions, but I knew Jill wouldn't answer them. She considered floral orders as confidential as a confession and had told me so in an earlier conversation shortly after she opened the shop. While she wrapped my order in tissue paper and added two dozen stems of flowers, my eyes strayed to the square paper Michael Wilson left on the counter. I strained to read the handwritten note upside down and backwards: R-U-E-S-N-A-D DANSEUR

From my early study of ballet, I remembered the French word for a male ballet dancer. Apparently, the stories of his frequent bouquets to Betty were true. I made a mental note of the word so I could ask Betty about it the next time we spoke.

I didn't mention the encounter to Nellie when I returned to the car. The threatening phone call weighed heavily on my mind, but I didn't want to ruin the evening by announcing it to everyone.

I thought about my wonderful group of acquired friends, who gave their time so generously whenever I needed them. These ladies could accomplish almost anything they set their minds to.

How dare the chief imply we were only a bunch of old women.

Sharon arrived early, putting out party napkins with a bold message: STRIKE WHILE THE IRON IS HOT. She set her pie on the table near the napkins.

Nellie laughed when she saw them. "Where do you find these things?" she asked. "You never fail to have a napkin to match the occasion."

Sharon shrugged. "It's what I do."

"Well, it's perfect," Nellie said.

When Harvey saw the napkins, he shook his head in amazement. "You women think of everything."

Tim stood the display walls and lattice upright so we could see how the booth would look when assembled. We oohed and aahed over his work until he told us to get busy with our part.

Kate assigned each of us a task, and we went immediately to work. There was no time to waste. Nellie prepared the sconces, filling them with flowers or candles. Sharon put plants into the planters, and sorted cookbooks for the bookstands. Kate and I gathered the signs and tied price tags to every item. We all supervised the men as they loaded everything into the back of Tim's pickup and Nellie's SUV. Moe dozed in the corner, staying out of everyone's way. That extra walk must have taken all his energy.

We talked as we worked. The conversation moved to Betty, and Kate wondered aloud why the Hamiltons had relocated to English Village, with Betty leaving behind a successful career in New York City. She looked to me for an answer.

"I don't know," I said. "She never gave me a direct answer to that question. But it isn't easy to be a dancer in a professional ballet company. Similar to career athletes, dancers generally reach their peak by thirty-five, and age out in their early forties. The practice and performance schedules are grueling, especially for lead dancers. It takes a serious toll on their bodies—particularly the women, who have to watch their weight so their partners can easily lift them into the air."

Nellie must have heard something wistful in my voice because she pounced on the comment. "Are you speaking from experience?"

I smiled at her. "Not exactly. I tried many years ago, but I didn't make the cut. I studied ballet all the way through high school and was serious about pursuing a career in dance—until I applied for a college program and was told I was far too short."

"That's terrible." Sharon came to stand beside me. "You are not short—just a little height-challenged, like me."

I laughed at her description. "Is that even a word? At this stage, I'm also far less flexible and a bit too old to entertain the idea of dancing."

"Nonsense." Harvey interrupted the conversation, giving me a look that sent tingles down my spine. "There are other kinds of dancing, you know. And you are definitely *not* too old."

"Says the youngster in the room."

Nellie raised her eyebrow at me, and Kate came to the rescue with a question about the murder investigation. "Have you heard anything new from the chief since we saw him this morning?"

I hesitated for a fraction too long.

"Well?" Kate prompted.

"Yes…" I dragged the word out into three syllables while I thought about what I should tell them. "There was an incident this afternoon, and Chief Marshall stopped by my house for a brief conversation."

"Well, for goodness sake, what was it?" Sharon came to my side and took my hand.

"It was really nothing. Someone called my cell. He disguised his voice, and he told me to stop asking questions about Bob's death."

"He threatened you?" Kate's normally calm voice went up an octave.

"He, um, suggested that we end our investigation, or someone might get hurt."

The room erupted with questions, and I had to calm everyone down. "Really, ladies, it was most likely a prank call from some kid who wants attention. The call was less than fifteen seconds, and he didn't make any clear threat."

"It sounds like a threat to me." Sharon put her hands on her hips, looking every bit like a feisty rooster ready to take on the world.

"Me too." Nellie's earrings bobbed as she nodded.

"Well, Chief Marshall coached me on some extra security measures, and I feel safe."

"Still, we need to watch out for each other," Nellie stated, calm and practical, as always. "Do you and Moe want to come and stay with us tonight?"

I tried to downplay the incident, so my friends wouldn't be concerned. "No, I will be fine." The chief thinks he is getting closer to solving the murder; it will all be over soon."

By nine, everything was packed and ready—boxes covered the table and the shop floor. We knew the display would be quick and easy to set up in the morning. We sat inside to rest for a few minutes, and Harvey gazed fondly around our little band of friends. He stood to get our attention.

"I want to say thank you to all of you. I never could have imagined a booth like this, and you've made it possible."

Nellie was the first to respond. She tucked her hair behind one ear and smiled up at him. "It was a team effort. When we saw the hours—and the skill—you put into making these awesome products, we wanted to be a part of it."

The rest of us chimed in, agreeing with her. Sharon spread her arms wide, indicating the full table of sale items. "This is a fun project for a worthwhile cause. It's our pleasure to help. We want your display to be the best one at the Summer's End Festival."

"Thank you." Harvey let his gaze rest on each person around the table. "I'm privileged to benefit from all your imagination and hard work. Now, let's all get out of here and get some rest. We have to be downtown to set up the booth in less than ten hours."

As we returned to the cars, I realized there was no longer room for Moe and me to fit into Nellie's vehicle. The back seat was stuffed to the ceiling with boxes for the display.

I shrugged and fastened Moe's leash onto his collar. "No worries. Moe and I will walk home. It's only a few blocks."

Harvey shook his head. "That's not happening. You can't be alone, at night, with a murderer still on the loose. I'll walk with you."

"I'd be happy to have your company." My supply of courage was mostly superficial, and I figured it wouldn't hurt to have a lanky blacksmith by my side. Besides, I had promised the chief I wouldn't walk around town by myself.

It was a warm summer evening, and the sky was a purple-blue, hovering between dusk and darkness. The meadow beyond the village park filled with fireflies blinking their way in slow motion, nice and low against the grass. I pointed to the field. "Look, Harvey. They're putting on a light show."

We stood, entranced, for a few minutes, watching nature's magical performance. "Even the cicadas are humming an accompaniment," Harvey whispered, as though he feared breaking the spell.

Standing beside him, I kept my voice low to match his. "I remember catching the lightning bugs and putting them in a Mason jar when I was a little girl visiting my grandmother here. We ran barefoot in the cool grass. Three little girls from the neighborhood, and me, competing to see how many fireflies we could gather."

"That sounds like a happy childhood." Harvey smiled down at me. "Did you poke holes in the top of the jars, so they could breathe?"

I nodded at him. "We did. But we never kept them for long. They were far too beautiful to stay locked in a jar."

We watched the show, entranced, for several more minutes. Moe stood between us, staring across the field as though he, too, enjoyed the entertainment.

The sweltering heat of the day had cooled, but the temperature still hovered in the low eighties. I looked up at Harvey. "This is one of the things I love about living in a small town. You would never see such a sight in the city."

We turned again to walk toward the cottage. Harvey talked as we walked, telling me about his decision to return to English Village and keep the family business running. "Our hardware store began as a grain and supply store back in 1919. My father took it over from his father. It seemed natural for me to follow in their footsteps."

"I'll bet your customers are second and third-generation families too."

He nodded. "We see everyone in the hardware store. Often, people tell me stories about my grandfather. Did you know he used to give a stick of Juicy Fruit gum to every child who came into the store? It was his favorite, so he figured kids would like it too. I always gave it to me, but it wasn't until I was older that I discovered he offered a stick to every kid who came in the door."

"Do you still do that?"

"I restarted the tradition earlier this year." He smiled and handed me a stick of gum from his pocket. "I have to clear it with their parents first. But today's kids seem to like it as much as my generation did."

"Seems like a simple way to make every child feel special."

We made it home in no time. Harvey took my hand in both of his at the door. "You be careful, Jo. I'm not leaving here until I know your door is locked up tight."

"Thanks, Harvey." I smiled at him as I closed the door.

"Call me if you need anything."

"I have Moe. See you tomorrow morning."

That night I slept fitfully, dreaming there was a shadow chasing me. I woke after midnight at the sound of a loud bump against the cottage wall. Could it have been the wind, knocking a tree limb into the window? I sat straight up in bed. Listening.

Moe, who normally snored through the night, now paced the floor, alternating between nudging me and whining at the back door. He heard something, too.

"What is it, Moe?" My voice came out in a whisper.

After several seconds of silence, I followed him to the door and peeked through the window. There was something on the back deck. I saw a shadow but could not make out the shape.

Whoever had delivered the package had also knocked out the porch light. Broken glass scattered in slivers across the wooden planks. My heart raced as I strained to see what was there.

It looked like a box, but I would swear I saw it move. I grabbed my cell to call the chief. The screen was black. The phone was dead. How could I have forgotten to charge it? Ducking below the windows, I raced to the front door and switched off my porch light. Then, Moe and I cowered into a corner behind the couch.

After five tense minutes with no sound but my own ragged breathing, I grabbed a flashlight from the kitchen drawer and followed Moe to the back door again – still hunkered down like the actors in every cop movie I'd ever watched. The suspense was too much for me. I figured if anyone was going to kill me, they would have battered the door down by now.

With Moe by my side, I turned the lock and opened the door, aiming the flashlight at the mysterious box. An unfamiliar order assailed my nose, and Moe scrambled out the door, barking like he meant business. He reached the box seconds before I realized what it was—a chicken crate filled with hens, flapping their wings like crazy at the sides of their cage. Feathers flew from the openings. There was a note attached to the top.

Summoning all the courage I had, I tiptoed outside to the center of the deck and grabbed the note from the cage. Moe barked sharply at the hens, who cackled and flapped harder, sending more feathers flying over the deck.

As I dragged Moe back inside and locked the door, I heard the bleep of a siren in my driveway. The cavalry had arrived.

Minutes later, Chief Marshall sat at my kitchen island. I poured him a cup of coffee, two sugars, no cream, and handed him the note:

CALL OFF YOUR BIDDIES.

The chief rubbed his forehead. "Who knew about our conversation?"

"No one."

"Someone did."

"I might have mentioned it to Kate."

"The marine?"

"Yes."

"And who did she tell?"

"I don't know."

The chief scowled at me across the table. He held the note in his hand. "I will find out who did this. Now, go charge your phone and get some rest."

The officers took the chicken crate with them. Moe snored on his bed in the corner of my room. I tried to sleep, but I largely tossed around in bed, my head full of questions. I woke early with a nagging feeling that I knew who killed Bob. But try as I might, I could not connect the dots in my mind. I hoped Chief Marshall would solve the case soon.

This old biddie wanted her life back.

Chapter Thirteen

Saturday morning promised to be another hot day. My weather app said the humidity factor would be high, as well. I could have predicted the humidity without a forecaster—my naturally curly hair spiraled into unruly tendrils before I left the house. I tied it back into a messy bun and added a straw hat and my sunglasses. I looked like a character out of a Laura Ingalls Wilder book, but at least my hair wouldn't be sweating against the back of my neck.

I put Moe on his leash and unlocked the door. Chief Marshall stood waiting for me.

"I told you to check the peephole before you opened your door."

"It's broad daylight. I have Moe beside me, and there will be hundreds of people on the streets this morning. Surely I'm safe?"

The chief sighed. "Criminals sometimes defy logic. Mind if I walk with you?"

If I hadn't considered the chief a friend, I might have resented the police escort. But we talked easily, and I was glad to have his company.

"About last night…" he started.

"Yes?"

"I'm sorry I called your friends 'biddies' that day. It was wrong, and I regret it."

"It's okay. I shouldn't have mentioned it to Kate."

He looked at me, and I could see the guilt on his face. "I may have mentioned it to a few people as well," he confessed. "I was still grumbling about your nosy friends and your fancy-pants reputation as a crime solver when I went back to the station."

"I have a fancy-pants reputation?" I smiled at the chief.

We walked together without speaking all the way to the corner. Then he turned to me again. "We're checking for fingerprints on the crate and note. And the lab will do a handwriting analysis."

"You'll find him."

"Let's agree that you'll keep this biddie episode to yourself."

"I won't say a word." And I meant it. Even though the Mahjong Mavens would consider it a declaration of war.

"Someone expects a reaction. It's best that we don't give it to him."

I couldn't resist asking about the murder case. "Do you have any new leads?"

"I might have a person of interest. If my new information turns into anything actionable, I'll bring him in for questioning."

I noted his reference to a male suspect and felt relieved that Betty might no longer be on his list.

"Meanwhile, I want you to pay attention to your surroundings," he continued. "Let me know if you see anything that doesn't look right to you."

"Like what?"

He shrugged. "You'll know it when you see it. Trust your instincts and call me if there's something amiss. Do not check it out yourself. You have my number. I want you to use it."

As we approached Main Street, I looked up at the chief by my side. "I'd hate for anything to ruin the Summer's End Festival. This is a big day for our little village."

"I'm aware of that." The chief rolled his eyes. "I'll try not to create a scene on Main Street." He tipped his hat as he turned to enter the police station. "Be safe, Josie."

I passed a dozen booth spaces before I arrived at Harvey's assigned location. Nellie was already there, helping Tim and Terry unload the display frame. Moe trotted over to sit under the shade of a large oak tree. I poured water from my water bottle into his portable dog bowl, placing it under the tree for him. I scratched his head before joining the others at the booth.

"You're just in time," Nellie said, handing me a roll of masking tape and one end of the banner. "Sharon walked up the block to Cozy Cups for take-out coffee. She should be back in a few minutes."

I looked at the surrounding booth spaces, all in varying stages of completion. "Wow. We're going to need a lot of visitors to buy from all of these exhibitors."

"We counted at least fifty vendors setting up on this strip of Main Street," Nellie said. "The road is blocked off from the park all the way to the other side of the City Building. Cars are already parked near the library and along the street west of the elementary school. They won't let shoppers enter until the booths are ready for business at nine. It looks to be our biggest Summer's End Festival ever."

Sharon rounded the corner of Harvey's booth, carrying cardboard containers of coffee. She placed one of the cups in my hands. "Ladies, let's get this party started. We have a lot of work to do."

Kate arrived from the opposite direction, carrying a box she set on the counter. "I have the calculator, a cash bag, and change."

She pulled a smaller container from the box. "And I brought extra price tags, markers, and thumbtacks."

Tim and Terry set the last brace in place and gave the booth frame a shake. "Looks solid to me," Tim said. "We'll move our truck out of the way so Harvey can pull in here with his merchandise. Then, you ladies can work your magic with the display."

Nellie motioned for me to step behind the lattice panel, and I knew what was coming. "Tell me what happened last night."

My pulse quickened before I realized she couldn't possibly know about the crate of chickens on my back deck. I looked at her as innocently as I could manage.

"I have no idea what you mean."

"Oh, yes, you do, Josie Posey. Harvey walked you home last night. Did he ask you out?"

I laughed at the expression on her face. "Of course not. He was a perfect gentleman. We're friends, Nellie."

"You are hopeless." She gave me an exaggerated eye roll and returned to the front of the booth.

Harvey was there, lifting boxes of his iron art out of his truck, and we all began to set the pieces into place. I was proud of the Mahjong Mavens. Together, we turned the booth into a masterpiece worthy of Harvey's art. As we stood back to survey the results, Harvey gave us a big happy grin and called us in for a group hug.

"We're going to make a big profit for the English Village Art Foundation." Harvey set another container of cookbook racks on the table, lifting the heavy box with ease. "And it wouldn't have happened without you."

"There is still work to be done," Kate reminded us. She gave me a pointed look. "Let's not count our chickens yet. Right, Josie?"

She laughed, but I felt the blood drain from my face.

Did Kate know about the crate of chickens? I had promised the chief I wouldn't mention them.

"Are you okay, Josie?" Kate asked. "You look a little pale."

Ahh. Suddenly I realized my friend had mentioned chickens as a private joke between us. It was a reference to the chief's earlier "biddies" comment I had shared only with her.

I gulped my coffee and brushed her concerns aside. "I'm fine. I didn't sleep well last night. All I need is a little caffeine."

Promptly at 9 a.m., the Village Fire Department flashed its lights, and the gates opened to shoppers. As the crowd increased, I decided to walk Moe back home. He loved the additional attention, but the heat would soon be too much for him. Even with his beautiful fluffy coat sheared to about an inch for the summer, Moe needed to be indoors for the hottest part of the day. Sharon and I were scheduled to help at the library book sale from 10–11 a.m., so we left the others to tend to Harvey's customers and strolled toward my cottage.

Sharon maneuvered between the booths as we steered Moe through the crowded sidewalks. "Look at all of these people," she said.

Literally dozens of shoppers were lined up to peruse handmade jewelry, scented candles, tie-dyed T-shirts, and more for sale at the booths. Mr. Nutter's food truck looked busy, and it was way too early for lunch. We passed a display of hand-blown glass from one of Harvey's fellow artisan friends. Then, I noticed a Swedish booth sponsored by the neighboring town of Lindsborg. They attended each year to promote their fall festival for those who might be interested in a day trip. I appreciated the friendly atmosphere between the two communities.

We paused for a few minutes at Barbara's Pet Stop booth, and I convinced Sharon to pick up some *Cheesy Pleasy* scones for her dogs, Thelma and Louise. She couldn't resist buying a package of Barbara's new Sticky Paws Peanut Butter biscuits, too. Sharon laughed as she draped the shopping bag over her arm. "This could be an expensive day for me."

My friend served on the board for this event, so I peppered her with questions. "Tell me again how the festival raises money. I know it goes to the Art Foundation, but what do they do with it?"

Sharon pointed to various booths along the route. "Every one of these vendors pays for a rental space. The booth fees cover our cost and generate enough money for the committee to promote the festival throughout our region. But for every dollar of merchandise they sell, the vendors give thirty cents to the foundation. So, if Harvey sells $2,000 worth of items, he will pay $600 to the foundation."

"With this many booths, that formula could generate a sizeable contribution."

"It does. Last year, the festival raised more than $50,000. The money supports a weekend art workshop for kids 8–18. We bring in guest artists, pay for art supplies, and host the students for a variety of classes. It all takes place one weekend in October. Nellie chairs that event."

"How many students attend?"

"Kids come from across the country. The private college in Lindsborg sponsors the breaks and hosts a booth where advisors can meet with older students about enrolling in the university arts curriculum or applying for scholarships."

"Betty mentioned the Fine Arts Workshop when I interviewed her," I noted.

"That must be what she was referring to. She planned to offer an introductory dance class. She even talked Michael into helping her. He agreed to teach a class of young boys the importance of being physically fit to become a male dancer. The sessions were supposed to demonstrate ballet, tap, and jazz. I wonder if they will still try to offer those."

"Might be canceled."

"I don't know," I said. "If it isn't until October, this murder thing will be behind us."

"Unless Michael is arrested," Sharon pointed out. "Isn't he a prime suspect?"

"He's on the list. One of many."

We dropped Moe at home and arrived at the library in time for our shift. I was relieved to see they had moved the used book sale to a shady location. The folding tables were heavy with books, already sorted into categories.

I smiled when I saw how neatly the books were labeled. Our librarian, Pam Williams, was a master at organization. She directed me to the center of the book sale.

"This is your section, Josie. I know you like mysteries and thrillers. Sharon is assigned to three tables of health and family books."

"Thank you, Pam. I'm looking forward to it."

I scanned the crowd. Other volunteers covered historical fiction, politics, children's books, and cookbooks. Sharon called out to me as she walked toward her section. "There must be five thousand books on these tables," she said.

"If we sell each of them for a dollar, we'll make a decent profit for the library and for the Art Foundation," I said. "Let's see what we can do."

For the next hour, I chatted with friends and neighbors while they browsed through the mystery books. One young girl came in search of a mystery about teenagers. I suggested several titles to her. The girl took three books, and I had a feeling she would devour them in short order.

I remembered summers with Grandma Molly when I was about twelve; I read every Nancy Drew mystery I could get my hands on. For three summers straight, I discovered new worlds through books—all to my grandmother's delight.

As the crowd milled around my table, I observed them carefully, trying to spot anyone who might have made the threatening phone call or delivered a brood of chickens to my door. The more I thought about it, the more I realized the caller had to be someone with access to my cell phone number. That ruled out most anyone who was a stranger to the village.

Again, I hoped the chief would find our murderer soon. As it turned out, I didn't have to wait much longer.

Chapter Fourteen

After our shift at the book sale, Sharon and I walked back to Harvey's booth. I saw his sign from a block away: HARVEY'S HANDCRAFTED METAL ARTWORKS. There were at least ten people gathered at the front of the booth. As we drew closer, I realized five of them were in line to pay for their purchases.

Kate took money and made change. Sharon visited with customers inside the booth, chattering away about cookbooks and pie baking. I could hear her instructing a young mother: "Oh no, dear, you must never use a store-bought pie crust. Use this recipe. It is easy to make, and your pies will be *much* better. Remember to use ice-cold water—that's the secret to a perfect crust."

Nellie restocked sconces and decorative mirrors, arranging them carefully on the shelves. She had a basket of fresh flowers beside her and a small box of candles. As I entered the booth, she called me to her side. "I think the sconces with flowers in them are selling faster than the candle sconces. So, I'm replacing all the candles with flowers."

Above it all was Harvey's beautiful chandelier. Secretly, I had imagined it hanging over my grandmother's antique table, but the price tag was marked boldly in red: SOLD. It was probably for the best. The piece was worth far more than I could afford to pay.

Harvey was positioned to the side of the booth entrance. I watched him for a moment, smiling and nodding at the small group gathering round him. He looked relaxed and happy, leaning down to speak to a young woman who clearly admired his work. She placed her hand on his arm, smiling into his eyes as she asked her question. I felt a pang of jealousy at her intimate gesture.

Then, another customer edged his way forward. "Your art is remarkable," he said.

I listened as the short, redheaded gentleman shook Harvey's hand and spoke enthusiastically about his display. The admirer wore a dapper bow tie, even in our late-summer heat. I felt a flicker of recognition as I stared at him from the back of the booth. "I had no idea you created this kind of work," the man said.

Harvey grinned down at him. "Thank you. I'm glad you like it. I doubt that it will ever be in a gallery, but it's something I enjoy doing."

The man scribbled a note on the back of a card and gave it to Harvey. "Please take my card and give me a call. I might change your mind about that."

Harvey nodded and tucked the card in his shirt pocket. The redheaded man moved on to the next booth as another customer stepped up in the line. Our local blacksmith was incredibly popular.

Sharon assisted customers while I stepped behind the booth to help Nellie rotate the inventory. The boxes were well organized for an effort that had come together so quickly. I was impressed by how many of the smaller items were already sold. Nellie and I replenished the entire wall of sconces, and then I put out a dozen more mirrors and cookbook holders.

We had all agreed to leave the financial transactions in Kate's capable hands. Everything appeared to be running smoothly, despite the crowds milling through the streets. But Harvey pulled me aside shortly after the red-headed man left the booth.

"Sales have been great this morning, but I'm concerned about keeping all of this cash on hand." He spoke quietly, so the customers couldn't hear. "Could you take some of it to the bank?"

"I can do that," I said. "It's a quick walk down the block, and they're open until noon."

I joined Kate behind the booth where she handed me a zippered pouch. "There's over $5,000 in here, along with a deposit slip. Stash it in your handbag and walk directly to the bank. I'll see if Nellie can go with you.

Be aware of the crowd around you. This is the kind of gathering where a purse-snatcher might be tempted to grab a little cash of his own."

I shook my head. "Honestly, Kate, things like that don't happen here."

She raised an eyebrow. "Really? Clearly, we have a murderer in town. You don't think we might also attract a thief?"

Without further protest, I accepted the bag and tucked it into my purse.

Nellie and I walked together a few blocks to the bank. And that's why we were the only ones to witness an argument in the alley beside the bank. Nellie first heard the heated conversation as we passed, and she nudged me to stop at the corner and listen.

"It's that dog walker, arguing with Betty's assistant. Can you hear them?"

I strained to listen, but all I could catch were a few words. "I told you it was too much." The girl's voice was raised in anger.

The man was obviously trying to reason with her. His voice was calm and low. "We talked about it and agreed."

I stood with my back to the alley but leaned closer to hear the conversation. "I think she's complaining about something he charged her for," I whispered to Nellie. "Maybe his price for janitorial work at the studio was higher than Betty had authorized."

Nellie shook her head. "Seems like an odd place to discuss a disputed invoice."

"Let's take care of the money, and if the two of them are still in the alley when we walk back, we'll check on them."

By the time we made our deposit and returned, the alley was empty. And I had forgotten the entire episode when we reached Harvey's booth. There, the customers flowed steadily, and we stepped inside to help. I admired the way the Mahjong Mavens moved easily between demonstrating products and chatting with visitors. I shouldn't have been surprised. These ladies were genuinely comfortable helping others.

Things slowed a bit after the lunch hour rush. Nellie and I took our break then, making our way toward the park. Many of the out-of-towners walked alongside us in search of the food trucks that lined the parking lot. A local band played bluegrass music in the gazebo. Miss Betty's young dance students lined up for their performance.

Nellie and I stood in the short line at Mr. Nutter's food truck. We were late enough that his lunch crowd had dispersed. I chose a pulled pork sandwich, and Nellie ordered barbecued chicken. We surveyed the park as we waited for our order.

"Look at this crowd." Nellie motioned to the people milling through the park and spilling over onto the sidewalks.

"At least half of them are strangers. It feels like I'm in the city again."

The event organizers had arranged plentiful rows of folding lawn chairs for visitors to enjoy the afternoon entertainment. Nellie and I found seats about five rows back from the gazebo stage. We settled into them, balancing our sandwiches and drinks on our laps. I glanced around the shady park and spotted several familiar faces. Across to my left was Mayor Minter, smiling at the young man beside her. I thought he might be her grandson, Andrew, but I couldn't see him well enough from this distance to identify him clearly. A couple of rows in front of us sat Larry Fox with two of those terrier puppies he often walked around town. I tapped my foot to the music and turned again to Nellie. "What a great event."

"It's a little too hot." she fanned her face with the program booklet. "But, aside from the heat, it is perfect."

It was at that moment I heard the urgent wail of a police siren coming around the curved road into the park. Chief Marshall pulled up to the curb abruptly. He turned off the siren but left the flashing lights spinning atop his vehicle. Like me, the crowd appeared surprised by his entrance; but no one panicked. The chief walked briskly toward the gazebo. At first, I thought he was coming directly toward me. But he kept right on going, striding past us and stopping beside Larry Fox and the puppies. He took Larry by the arm, spoke urgently into his ear, and escorted the dog walker to the patrol car, puppies and all. They drove off without lights or siren.

The crowd talked excitedly about the incident for about thirty seconds, then returned to enjoying the entertainment. The little dancers stepped onto the stage under the guidance of her assistant Alyssa. I marveled at her poise. When the chief drove off with Larry, the young woman was flustered; her face was red, and she seemed ready to burst into tears. But she rallied quickly and gathered the young dancers into place for their performance. I guess she really did believe "the show must go on."

Still slightly stunned by the interruption, Nellie and I turned to each other. "What do you think just happened?"

"I don't know," I replied.

"Do you think the dog walker is the murderer?"

"I guess we'll have to wait and find out."

I wanted to leave the park and head down to Chief Marshall's office, but something told me I would not be welcome there. Now that my assignment for *The Village Gazette* had turned into a crime story, the chief had made our roles clear. His job was to investigate. Mine was to report the facts—and stay safe. He could ask me for information, but I wasn't to question him for details.

After the little dancers took their bows, I walked home to check on Moe. This time, I didn't worry about having someone escort me. I felt pretty sure that the chief had apprehended a suspect and that my life was not in danger. Harvey and the rest of the mavens had his booth under control. It was barely two o'clock, but I was exhausted; my mind was spinning and my feet hurt. I needed a few minutes to think about this new development.

Safely inside, Moe stretched across the floor in front of the couch and rested his head on my feet, waiting for me to process the afternoon's events. My sweet dog always knew when I needed him. If only humans were as perceptive as dogs. Maybe we would be better at solving mysteries, I thought.

It was hard for me to see Larry as a murderer. I couldn't figure out what he would gain by having Bob dead. At 2:15 p.m., the chief called. "If you can stop by the station this afternoon, I'm happy to share some news about a person of interest for your report."

"I was in the park when you came for Larry Fox. Is he your suspect?"

"That's what I want to discuss, Josie. I've also got some questions you may be able to answer. Things your interviews may have uncovered."

"I'll be there in ten minutes." I ended the call, but my head was reeling with theories.

Could the dog walker have some other grudge against Bob Hamilton? Did Betty have a stronger connection with the man than she had admitted?

Chapter Fifteen

My meeting with the chief was short and sweet. He ushered me into the same small room where he might have interrogated Larry Fox. "Please sit down, Josie."

He closed the door and turned to me with a serious look on his face. "Despite my desire to keep you out of this investigation for your own safety, we continue to cross paths. While I'm uncomfortable involving you, I now believe the department could benefit from a collaboration between us."

I waited for him to elaborate.

"This means I would brief you on our developments. In return, you would share your research with me. Frankly, our department is too small to move as quickly as I would like on this case. Your candid observations will provide a different perspective."

"Are there any conditions to this collaboration?" I asked.

The chief smiled. "Yes. You will maintain confidentiality on sensitive facts we uncover. Your full crime story would have to wait until the case is solved. Until then, you would report only the basic facts, as provided in official statements from our department."

I thought for only a moment before I agreed. "I'd be happy to assist you, if I'm able."

"Good." The chief nodded and reached out to shake my hand. "Welcome to the team." He sat across from me and folded his hands on the table. "I wanted to talk to you for two reasons. First, to let you know, we consider Larry Fox a person of interest in the murder of Bob Hamilton. I'll tell you why in a moment."

I nodded without speaking. The chief was wearing his official law enforcement hat, and his manner was all business. I didn't want to interrupt.

"Secondly, I don't want you to assume that you are off the hook when it comes to being mindful of your surroundings. Mr. Fox is our prime suspect right now, but he has not yet been arrested. Until that happens, you are to continue the security measures we put in place yesterday. Is that clear?"

"Yes," I answered without a trace of whining in my voice.

The chief continued with his briefing. "Mr. Fox is a suspect because we found a heated exchange of emails going back and forth between the dog walker and Bob Hamilton."

"Did he threaten to kill him?"

"Not specifically. But they are abusive and intimidating in nature." Chief Marshall sat across from me, leaning his arms on the old metal table. "It's enough to prove he was angry. The words imply that Bob should be punished, but they don't directly threaten murder."

"Is there anything else?"

"Yes." Chief Marshall sighed heavily. "We found a blistering review Bob posted on social media complaining about the dog walker. That likely cost Mr. Fox a great deal of business."

"Betty told me she and Bob never actually hired Larry to walk their dog. I wonder why she said that. How could Bob give the dog walker a review if they never used him?"

"You'll understand when you see the printouts." The chief tapped his pen on the table. "Bob's comments don't claim that Larry was negligent with Tinkerbelle. They imply the dog walker couldn't be trusted to keep pups out of harm's way."

"He suggested that Larry wasn't a competent dog walker?" I pushed away from the table and stood to pace the floor.

"Bob's review was more direct than that. He essentially called Larry an idiot who should not be trusted to care for man's best friend—even for short periods of time. The review states Bob's opinion was based on his conversations with Larry and on his actions when the dog walker took Tinkerbelle for very brief 'get-acquainted' walks twice in a two-week period.

Both of those walks he performed at no charge to the Hamiltons."

I stopped pacing and stared at the chief. "We're basing a murder charge on bad business reviews and a heated argument about a dog getting into a flowerbed?"

The chief rubbed his chin. "It's all we have right now. I agree it isn't enough."

I thought for a moment before I asked the question I knew the chief anticipated. "You believe Larry may have had a motive or a desire to harm Bob, but there's nothing to support that he took an action. Is that what you're saying?"

"We have no information yet about the poison, so we can't connect Mr. Fox to that. However, he lied to us about the severity of the disagreement between them. And, he had more contact with their dog, Tinkerbelle, than he admitted in our initial conversations."

"Which means he may have had an opportunity to be in Bob's house, where he could poison his food. If he took a couple of complementary walks with Tinkerbelle, Larry could have been at their home at least three times," I surmised.

"Yes, Josie. And there's one more thing." The chief paused to make certain he had my full attention.

"What?"

"I visited with Mr. McGregor at the Curiosity Shop to see what kind of employee Larry is. I wanted to know more about his temperament and work ethic."

"And?"

"McGregor considers Larry an ideal employee. He shows up on time. He pays attention to details. He does a meticulous job cleaning the antique clocks and winding them. He also helps clean the floors and take out the trash."

"That doesn't sound like a murderer. It sounds like an exemplary employee. He takes out the trash for Miss Betty's School of Dance, too. He works hard, making ends meet."

"I agree." The chief had an aggravating way of circling around a conversation before he came to the point.

"So?"

"McGregor also showed me the lab where Larry prepares the solvent he uses to clean the clocks. Some of those products include toxic chemicals. Larry has become somewhat of an expert on mixing a specially formulated clock-cleaning solution for antique clocks. The process is tedious since it requires each clock part to be polished separately. If they aren't cleaned properly, residue will build up, and the clock is no longer operable."

"The formula is deadly?"

"It isn't your typical arsenic, but yes. Larry's off-hours of work at the Curiosity Shop give him access to some potent specialized cleaning products used only for those antique grandfather clocks. We're waiting to see if the coroner's report will link the poison in Bob's system to the chemicals in Mr. McGregor's formula."

"I hadn't considered a cleaning solution as a poison, but it makes sense."

"McGregor said Larry always preferred to mix his own solvent, particularly since clocks made before 1820 require a different solution than those made after that year. For the older clocks, he used an ammonia-free solution; but the newer ones required high concentrations of liquid ammonia along with some other chemicals. It can be highly poisonous if ingested."

"This could be the evidence you need, to connect Larry to Bob's murder."

"Either way, there's something off-kilter about Larry's story. I can't figure out what it is. Right now, I don't have enough to hold him, so you may see him around town."

"Should I talk to him?" I asked.

"Absolutely not. One of the reasons I'm sharing this with you is to protect you. If he is the murderer, he won't take kindly to anyone who threatens to expose him. Act normal and enjoy the rest of the Summer's End Festival."

"Right. Act normal. I'll do my best, Chief. I left the police station and walked back down Main Street, browsing through the booths to see what I could discover. Nothing took my mind off the murder. Instead, I looked over my shoulder and watched for Larry Fox to appear in the crowd. I wondered how I could act normal when I was afraid to see him.

A woman's display of handmade dog toys caught my eye, and I bought a small stuffed Lamb Chop sheep for Moe. She was cute, with bright red lips and long eyelashes. It made me smile to think of my sweet Old English sheepdog playing with a little sheep of his own. He already had a basketful of toys, but I knew he would love this addition.

It was nearly three when I returned to Harvey's display. Kate greeted me with a hug. "Bless you. We haven't had a lunch break yet. Can you handle the cash register?"

"Sure. I'm good for at least three hours. Show me how to work the phone thingy for credit cards."

She gave me a lesson and watched as I processed my first customer's card. Then, Kate and Sharon were off, leaving me in the booth with Harvey and Nellie.

Nellie hurried to my side. "I told everyone what happened at the park over lunch. Have you heard anything from the chief?"

I nodded. "Yes. I stopped at the station on my way here. It's...complicated. Let's take care of these customers, and I'll fill you in later."

We worked the rest of the afternoon, selling and restocking Harvey's ironwork pieces. The crowd thinned during the heat of the afternoon, but his sales were steady. By five, only a few pieces remained. We spread everything onto one table and pulled it forward to the front of the booth.

At six, the whole gang returned to clear out the merchandise. Harvey packed up the chandelier and five unsold pieces. The booth frame could stay where it was until Tim and Terry showed up for teardown around eight. Most of us were planning to gather at the gazebo later for the concert and fireworks. Harvey thanked us for our help, then took his remaining inventory back to his shop.

The rest of us walked together to Mr. Nutter's food truck for a quick dinner. My phone app confirmed I'd already walked 15,000 steps, so I splurged on a foot-long hot dog and a hand-squeezed lemonade. Exhausted, we shared a picnic table—and devoured the food in front of us. While we ate, I gave everyone the highlights of my conversation with the chief.

"It must be hard to have a suspect but not be able to arrest them." Sharon sat her chicken sandwich on the tray in front of her and moved her fries closer to me. "I hope he is able to gather the evidence he needs soon."

"Me, too." I reached for one of her fries.

None of us could imagine the dog walker as a murderer. Kate was the first to say it. "Larry is a young guy who likes dogs. I don't see him killing anyone."

"Maybe not." I snatched another french fry. "But the chief considers him a prime suspect. He told me not to judge a book by its cover when it comes to murderers."

"Well, I'd pick the marine before I would think of the dog walker." Kate's matter-of-fact observation was met with a chorus of protests from the rest of us.

"You're the one who said Thomas Fisher couldn't have done it." I waved Sharon's french fry in Kate's face.

"I said he wouldn't have used poison. But he would be more capable of killing someone than Larry."

"Now, I'm really confused." I wiped my hands with a napkin and shoved Sharon's tray farther away.

We cleared the table and gathered our things. Kate and I had decided to take Bacon and Moe with us for the music in the park. We left the others to retrieve our pets, parting at the corner of Primrose Lane. I told my friend goodbye. "You go on. I can make it from here. It's two blocks."

With the crowd still milling about and a bright sun shining overhead, I wasn't worried about walking alone to get Moe. That is, not until I turned the corner and saw Larry Fox coming directly toward me.

Chapter Sixteen

How had I gone so quickly from the safety of crowded Main Street onto the desolation of Persimmon Road? For a moment, I panicked. I remembered Larry arguing with Alyssa in the bank's alley. Then I imagined him at Mr. McGregor's, mixing solvents from toxic chemicals. I took a deep breath as the dog walker came toward me on the sidewalk.

"Hey, Ms. Posey," he called out to me from the corner, sauntering in my direction. "Have you been enjoying the Summer's End Festival?"

Remembering the chief's instructions to "act normal," I pasted a fake smile on my face. "Yes, how about you?"

Larry continued to approach me. My eyes darted to my cottage, judging the distance between us. There was no way for me to reach home before we crossed paths. He stopped a few feet in front of me, blocking the sidewalk.

"I saw part of the Festival, but Chief Marshall called me in to answer questions right in the middle of the noon entertainment."

My cheeks hurt from smiling. I switched to a slight frown I hoped looked natural. "What was that about?"

Larry shrugged and studied my face. He stepped closer. "I guess he thought I could tell him something new about Bob Hamilton. But I barely knew the guy."

I tossed my head and laughed a totally "normal sounding" laugh. "Well, I wouldn't worry about it. The chief called me in too. He's talking to everyone who might have spoken to Bob or Betty in the past couple of weeks."

The dog walker's eyebrows shot upward. "Oh. That makes sense, then."

I nodded back at him, my head bouncing like one of those bobblehead toys on car dashboards. "He's very thorough. That guy asks a lot of questions."

Larry visibly relaxed, and then he leaned toward me. "I have to admit I was nervous. I had a run-in with Mr. Hamilton over some stupid flowers, and then he gave me a bad review on my website. I was afraid the chief would think I killed the guy over it."

"That would be a pretty big reaction to a bad review." I laughed again, louder and longer. Larry laughed along with me, like I'd said something hilarious, so I guessed I fooled him. "It sure would. I'm trying to build a business, so reviews are important. But I'm not going to murder a guy for posting or bad one or yelling at his own pet."

I forced another laugh. "Of course not."

Larry grinned at me. "I might rough him up a little. But I'd never kill him."

I felt my eyes widen, and I spoke more quietly. "You might not want to say that out loud to the chief."

"Sorry. I was kidding, but I guess it's not smart to joke about murder."

I decided to make my escape while I had the opportunity. "Well, I'm headed home to get Moe now. Enjoy the rest of the festival."

He waved, and I hurried to get into the cottage. My knees were shaking as I locked the door behind me. I could see Larry turn back toward Main Street at the end of Persimmon Road.

Moe met me at the door. I gave him a hug that was more for me than for him. "You won't believe how frightened I was. It's good to see your friendly face." I pulled the new lamb toy from my shopping bag and handed it to him before I poured myself a big glass of iced tea. Moe immediately carried the toy to his favorite rug, resting his paw on her face.

The concert was scheduled to begin at dusk. I had time to shower and change; the water soothed my nerves and calmed my overactive imagination to the point that I decided Larry Fox couldn't be a killer.

I chose a sleeveless summer dress with bright sunflowers printed across the flowing skirt and soft yellow sandals. Then I added a pair of dangling earrings and my favorite gold bracelet. A glance in the full-length mirror told me what I wanted to know: The dress looked flattering and festive without being too "flirty." Even at my age, I wanted to feel feminine.

I couldn't remember the last time I looked forward to something as much as this evening. We had worked hard the last several days, and I was ready to relax and enjoy the music under a starlit summer sky. The featured band was a low-key bluegrass group that promised to appeal to all ages. Glancing at my husband Ken's photo on the mantle, I felt the warmth of his smile. If he were here, he would remind me to enjoy every day.

The pile of note cards scattered over my dining room table called to me, but I ignored them. I had already spent so much time pondering the murder case that my brain felt dizzy. I kept spinning in circles from one suspect to another, unable to land on a single killer. It was time for a break.

I fastened Moe's leash, and we walked out the door.

Kate and Bacon met us at the corner. The two dogs had shared many playdates over the last couple of years. I still remembered when Kate named her pooch. She had tried several names, but the dog refused to come to anything. Finally, she called me one day with an announcement.

"I've named him Bacon," she practically shouted into the phone.

"Bacon?" I echoed, a little stunned by her choice.

"Yep. His name is Bacon. When I call out 'bacon,' he comes running. It's the only word he responds to."

I had laughed with her. "It's perfect."

Now, the four of us walked all over town together, and the name Bacon didn't sound strange at all.

Kate and I arrived at the gazebo area a few minutes before the concert began. All our mahjong friends were assembled. Harvey had saved a couple of seats for us, and we settled into them. A huge lump formed in my throat, and tears welled in the corners of my eyes, thankful for my little group of friends. Harvey turned toward me. "Are you okay, Josie?"

I swallowed the lump and nodded my head. "I'm fine, Harvey. I had a silly moment of emotion wash over me."

"Being happy is never silly."

"The people here are really special. I can see why my Grandma Molly loved English Village."

Harvey clasped his hands and leaned forward in his chair. "Most people think it's an ordinary small town in Kansas. I'm glad you see its charm."

As the band played, Harvey reached over to take my hand. "Now, I recall, you promised to dance with me."

"I don't recall that at all. I believe we were arguing about whether I was too old to dance."

"You are not too old." He stood, pulling me out of my chair alongside him. Kate took Moe's leash, and Harvey walked me to the dance area. We talked and laughed as he took me into his arms and waltzed across the grass.

As we returned to our seats, Nellie gave me one of her raised-eyebrow looks, but I ignored it. Harvey leaned toward me and cocked his head. "Josie, how old do you think I am?"

"Not old enough."

"No, seriously."

"I don't know. Maybe forty-eight?"

"I was in high school with Tim's brother Jimmy, and he is fifty-one."

"Yes, but you seem younger. I figure you probably skipped a grade or two."

Harvey gave me one of those big, happy laughs that came from deep inside him. "Actually, it's the opposite. I was a preemie-baby. I was still so small when it was time to start school that they held me back a year. And then, I got rheumatic fever in the second grade and was out sick for so long I had to repeat that grade. So, I'm fifty-three, Josie. I'll be fifty-four on my birthday in a few months. Is that old enough for you?"

"It certainly closes the gap. I turned fifty-five on my last birthday."

My sweet dog loved being around people, but fireworks made him tremble and whine. I always tried to get him into the house, safe and sound, before the noisy blasts began. Harvey walked with me to take Moe home before the fireworks began. We sat outside in my front yard, watching the showering lights from a distance. Afterwards, I said goodnight and carefully locked my doors, turning on the porch light as I had promised Chief Marshall I would.

Chapter Seventeen

Sunday morning, I was prepared to sleep in and skip church, but the sun rose at six, and Moe planted his face on the edge of my bed, nose-to-nose with mine. I opened my eyes to find him staring patiently back at me. When Moe gave me that look, I didn't argue. I crawled out of bed and pattered barefoot to let him out the back door.

When he returned, I let him in and reset the lock. We had a leisurely morning compared to the previous day. I read from the book I'd picked up for myself at the library book sale before my growling stomach urged me to make breakfast. On Sundays, I always shared my scrambled eggs and bacon with Moe—spreading his portion on top of his regular dog food. He finished it in record time.

I dressed for church and climbed into my car. The little red convertible was my one big splurge after my husband died. I preferred to walk about town when I could: It was good exercise, and Moe could accompany me. But, when the distance was too far, or I simply needed to move a little faster, I drove Piper. Occasionally, Moe hustled into the back seat of the VW "Bug" and we drove together with the top down, my hair and his ears blowing in the wind.

"Let's go, girl." I often spoke aloud to the little red vehicle as I did to Moe. She started right up, and I backed carefully out of the garage. Nearly every cottage on my street had an attached garage, unlike the true English villages in Great Britain. It was likely a concession to our ever-changing weather.

Whoever had planned the village, originally, had given more than a nod to the Cotswold District of England. Our streets and neighborhoods followed the same patterns as the quintessentially English market towns and villages from that region. Many of our homes were built from honey-colored native limestone, like the quaint cottages found in Burford or Castle Combe. Window boxes, overflowing with blossoms and ferns, adorned most of the cottages. I breathed in their fragrances as I made the morning drive.

It was a short distance past the park and beyond the library to the picturesque little chapel that still took my breath away. Built of native white limestone, the structure featured huge blocks that framed beautifully arched stained-glass windows. The church sat pristinely in the center of a lovely green garden. A tall steeple pointed majestically toward heaven, and a sweet bell tower sent echoes of my favorite hymns across the town. A sense of calm descended upon me as I found a parking space near the back entrance.

Inside the sanctuary, open-beamed ceiling soared above rows of antique wooden pews that spread outward from a center aisle. The handcrafted windows were spaced evenly along both sides of the chapel. Rainbows of light slanted across the room, casting a rosy glow on the gathered worshipers. I took my usual seat on the polished pew one row behind Nellie and Tim. Soon, Kate slipped into the pew beside me.

We had settled into a routine that began with our common interest in mahjong on Wednesdays, but soon included coffee shop excursions, walks with our dogs, and the traditional Sunday morning service at the English Village Chapel.

After the service, Pastor Pinkerton always stood near the exit shaking hands and chatting with his church family. Ahead of me, he spoke to one of our oldest citizens. "Nice to see you, Mary. How's George doing with that broken ankle?"

I walked down the broad stone steps and was surprised to see Chief Marshall waiting there for me. He stepped closer and leaned down to speak quietly. Nellie and Kate hovered nearby, but they weren't close enough to hear the chief's words.

"Josie, the coroner's report came back this morning. Bob's death was caused by poison, as predicted. Most likely administered through a batch of salsa. But the type of poison wasn't what I expected."

"What was it?"

"Bob Hamilton died from the toxic effects of several alkaloids in his body: lycorine, pancracine and amaryllidine."

"Are those ingredients in the clock-cleaning chemicals?"

"No. They are found in the bulb or sap of the Amaryllis belladonna plant—also known as the Jersey lily or Naked Lady flowers. Bob was poisoned by flower petals."

It took a moment for me to absorb this new information. "Could Bob have had too much direct contact with the flowers in his garden? Maybe it wasn't a murder at all?"

"Oh, it was murder, Josie." The chief frowned at me, his smooth ebony forehead folding into deep wrinkles above his thick eyebrows.

"Are you sure?" I asked, still unconvinced.

Death by flowers?

"The concentration levels found in his bloodstream would never have come from routine interaction with the flowers. He had to ingest a high dose of the flower. But not many people would know how poisonous the flower could be. And, even fewer would have access to put the concoction into Bob's food or drink. His wife is our obvious suspect."

"Wait. Betty offered me chips and salsa when I interviewed her. If the salsa was poisoned, I don't believe she knew it." I shook my head. "Besides, Sharon told me Betty never cooked, so it's unlikely she would have mixed it into the salsa or any other food."

The chief cleared his throat. "Well, I don't see how Larry could have done it. When we interrogated him, he had a sneezing spell. He said it was due to the fresh flowers on the receptionist's desk. The guy has a serious allergy. Took him 20 minutes to get it under control. I don't think he's our man."

"In my mind, there's only one person with the knowledge, the access, and a motive," I said.

"Michael Wilson."

Poor Betty. She's going to lose both men she cared for—one to murder, and the other to prison.

"I'll be bringing Michael in this afternoon. Please don't mention this to anyone."

We talked for a few minutes in the church parking lot before the chief headed back to his office. I felt sad to think of this tragic end to what I considered a beautiful love story.

Nellie and Kate caught up with me as I was about to drive out of the parking lot. "What can you tell us?" Kate was breathless from hustling to my side.

"Nothing, yet. Let's get together this evening, and I'll share anything I can by then. Chief Marshall is in the middle of a breakthrough on the case."

I went home and grabbed a pack of blank notecards from my kitchen drawer. With Moe at my feet, I scribbled random thoughts and questions onto each card, tossing them into another pile on the table. It seemed like a disorganized mess, but this system had always helped me clarify my theories in the past.

Now, going through my murder investigation notes, the cards fell into three categories: Motive (Why), Means (How), and Opportunity (When & Where). It wasn't enough to prove that a suspect had a reason to kill Bob. He had to have a way to accomplish the deed, and the opportunity to make it happen. After I had written all my questions onto cards, I began to turn them face-up, one by one.

Under Motives, I had three cards.

First: Jealousy. This was the obvious motive. Michael Wilson loved Betty. He had waited for her a long time and was tired of being second to Bob.

Second: Love. Everyone said Michael would do anything for Betty. Had something changed in Betty's relationship with Bob? Had she asked Michael to help her out of a difficult situation?

And Third: Hate. Perhaps Michael had simply grown to hate Betty's husband over time. Even a small incident could push the botanist to the point of harming Bob.

For Means, I had only one answer: Poison. We knew Bob was poisoned. As a botanist, Michael knew the toxic elements of the Naked Lady blossoms. He also knew they were abundant in the Hamiltons' garden.

For Opportunity, I had a stack of options: Michael was in the Hamilton home often. Michael knew the couple, and their food preferences. Michael was a trusted friend, so he could easily tamper with a favorite food or drink to administer the poison.

Is Michael Wilson capable of murder?

I pondered the question in light of all I knew about love and hate and jealousy.

My mind raced with this latest development. Poison-by-flower-petals. And I had the inside track on solving the murder.

Chapter Eighteen

I t didn't take long for word to spread that Michael Wilson had been arrested for the murder of his longtime adversary Bob Hamilton. My phone rang shortly after lunch, and I could barely hang up from one call before another came in.

First, it was Larry Fox. "Did you hear about the botanist? Chief Marshall called to thank me for answering his questions earlier. Then, he said he had arrested Michael Wilson as a suspect in Bob Hamilton's murder."

"Yes, I heard."

"I wanted to be sure you knew. I guess you were right; the chief is a smart guy who figured it out."

His call was quickly followed by three more from my mahjong friends. Kate simply said, "I know *you* know, but we want to talk about it. Are we still meeting at your house tonight?"

"Yes."

Nellie's call was even shorter. "Tonight, at six?"

"Yes."

And Sharon's was only a comment: "Don't eat. We're bringing dinner."

"I'll be here."

Midway through the afternoon, I took a call from Bob's marine buddy, Thomas Fisher.

"Josie Posey?" I knew it was the marine because he barked his question like a true commander.

I wanted to shout, "Yes, SIR," but I was afraid to offend him. Instead, I simply answered, "Yes."

"Sergeant Thomas Fisher. I hope it's okay to call?"

"Of course. What can I do for you, Sergeant Fisher?"

"Please, call me Thomas."

"What can I do for you, Thomas?"

"I heard you are writing an investigative story on my friend Bob's murder. If you need any additional background information, I'd be happy to help."

"Is there a reason you are calling me now?"

"Yes. I heard the news, and I think the chief did the right thing when he arrested Michael."

"If you know something related to the case, you need to talk to the chief yourself. This isn't my investigation; it's official police business."

"I don't know anything about the murder. All I'm telling you is that Michael has always wanted Betty and would go to any extreme to have her."

"I hear you, Thomas. But you understand the appropriate chain of command on this. If you have any details that point to Michael as the murderer, you need to call the chief. If it's information to clarify my crime story, I'm happy to hear it."

"Listen, Michael is the only person I know, other than Bob himself, who would have the capability to make a poison from the blooms of the Naked Lady flowers."

"I never mentioned what kind of poison the coroner identified."

The marine's laugh was a bark. "You didn't have to. It's a small town. Word gets around. Besides, I heard it earlier today from that dog walker. He agrees with me. Michael Wilson has to be the murderer."

"How do you know Larry Fox? I thought you were in town for a short visit with Mr. Hamilton."

The marine swore on the other end of the line. "I'm not an idiot, Ms. Posey. I've been in town a week, and I've seen the dog walker at several events. He left his business cards at the Philbrook Bed and Breakfast earlier this week. While he was there, we shared a lunch table. All he could talk about were two things: his dog walking business and my friend, Bob Hamilton's, murder."

"Tell me more about your friendship. How did the two of you meet? And when did you become acquainted with Michael Wilson?"

104

"You've probably heard the story already from Betty. Michael and I were roommates in college. Then, he took a year off to perform in the New York City Ballet. I enlisted in the United States Marine Corps. We were obviously two very different people."

"So, you knew Michael before you met Bob?"

"That's right. Bob Hamilton was in the Corps with me. He was older, but we served together for two years before we were stationed back in the States. We were both committed to serving our country."

"Were you around when Bob met Betty?"

"I sure was. I saw it happen. The New York City Ballet had a special performance night for enlisted officers. It was part of a Marine Corps Ball charity event. Our commanding officer wanted to show the military's support of the arts, so he suggested that we all go. Bob and I sat together. I'll never forget his face when he saw Betty dance onto that stage. He couldn't take his eyes off her."

"And Michael?"

"Imagine my surprise to see my former college roommate up there onstage with the prima ballerina. I knew he was in the dance company, but I didn't know he had a leading role."

"Everyone was at the ball together that night?"

"That's right. I went up to Michael after the performance. He introduced me to Betty. Then I introduced Bob to Betty. They became inseparable. It was as though the rest of us weren't even in the room. Bob insisted on taking Betty home that night, so I took a cab back on my own. The rest is history."

My next call was from Pastor Pinkerton. His caring tone nearly brought tears to my eyes. "Are you all right, Josie? I know you've been helping the chief with this case. Remember that when you get off a roller coaster, it's natural to feel a little dizzy."

I laughed at his analogy. "That's exactly how I'm feeling, Pastor. I'll be fine in a couple of days."

Finally, the chief called. "Josie, we arrested Michael Wilson this afternoon and will be charging him with first-degree murder. I thought you would want to know."

"Did he confess?"

"He confessed to everything but the murder. He admits he has always loved Betty, and he was jealous of Bob. He admits that he was often at their home, and he knew their eating habits."

"But he says he didn't kill Bob?" I added.

"It's an odd situation. He doesn't say he didn't. But he won't say he did."

"What about the poison?"

"When I told Michael about the type of poison identified in Bob's system, he didn't seem surprised. He said, as a botanist, he was aware of the toxicity of the Amaryllis belladonna flowers. He even admitted he knew how to grind the flowers and bulbs into a dry powder that could have been mixed into a food or drink to poison someone."

"Did he seem angry or upset as you questioned him?"

"It was more like he was resigned to the inevitable. He was calm. He was reasonable. He answered every question without asking for an attorney."

"Maybe he expected to be arrested?" I proposed.

The chief sighed before he continued. "I wish I felt better about the outcome, but I'm confident he's our guy."

"Did he tell you anything that only the murderer would know?"

"When I explained we had found traces of salsa ingredients in the deceased's stomach, Michael said it all made sense."

I was puzzled. "What all made sense?"

"He said Bob loved salsa, but Betty never touched it. She was allergic to tomatoes. Not many people knew that."

I reassured the chief that sometimes the logical suspect really is the guilty one.

"Yes," he agreed. "I guess he was tired of watching her with another man. He finally snapped and decided to kill his competition."

Still...something about the arrest seemed too easy. "So why won't he make it official? Shouldn't he confess?"

The chief sighed heavily. "I've seen this kind of thing before. Once I interviewed a prisoner on death row. He told me every detail of the murder. He explained that he hated the victim, that he bought a gun with the intent to shoot the victim, and that he tracked the victim's daily routine to determine the best time and place to kill him. But he recited it all as though he were observing it happen—or dreaming it happened. When I asked him to confess, he said, 'Oh, I saw it all. But I didn't do it.'"

"Do you think that's what happened here? Was Michael in the same kind of trance as he spoke to you?"

"It was the same, but different." The chief sounded as baffled as I was. "Michael is a scientist. He seemed to be calmly reviewing the facts and then analyzing the results. Oddly, he approached the murder as more of a theoretical event. He came to the same conclusion that I did, naming himself as the most likely suspect. But that was where it ended."

I stared out my window, trying to process the chief's explanation.

Finally, I repeated what I had heard. "He agreed he had the motive, the knowledge, the desire, and the means to commit the murder…but he doesn't admit doing it?"

"That's correct."

"Hmm…this is going to be an interesting trial."

"It is, indeed."

"I've been working this case non-stop for five days. We've made an arrest. We don't have to have a confession to get a conviction," Chief Marshall said, and I could hear the weariness in his voice. "It's time for a break. I'm going home to Lorene and Suzy. You should take a break too."

When he hung up, I turned to Moe. "What do you think, boy? The chief says we need a break. Shall we go for a walk?" I snapped the leash onto his collar, and we walked out the door.

By the time we reached the corner, one of those little bells rang in my head, and I knew this case wasn't solved. Yet.

Chapter Nineteen

Sharon arrived at 5:30 p.m., her arms wrapped around several bags of groceries and supplies. "I'm here to set the table and prepare a salad.

"Okay. But let me pour you a glass of wine," I offered.

"Perfect. I suppose you could also unwrap the eating utensils and paper plates." She directed me toward one of the bulging grocery bags. "Then give me a hand chopping these carrots."

I smiled. Sharon was a former second-grade school teacher. She knew how to give directions. When I unpacked the grocery bags, I had to laugh. Sharon had even thought to pick up fresh flowers.

Soon, the bouquet was centered on my grandmother's beautiful table. I set the paper plates on the end of the kitchen counter and separated the plastic forks, spoons, and knives, using the plastic cups Sharon provided as containers for the utensils.

We happily chopped side by side, and Sharon told me stories about her dogs, Thelma and Louise.

As we set the salad and dressings on the kitchen counter, Nellie came in carrying a huge casserole dish that smelled deliciously of lasagna. Soon after, Kate arrived with garlic bread and containers of iced tea.

Next, Sharon entered to applause as she placed a golden peach pie onto the counter—still warm from her oven.

"We will never eat all of this."

"But we're willing to try." Nellie laughed and began slicing the lasagna.

Everyone filled plates, and I realized we were missing napkins. I headed toward the pantry. "I'll get paper towels."

"No worries." Sharon put her hand on my arm, stopping me. "I came prepared."

She pulled a package of printed napkins from her purse and passed them around. "This was the closest I could find for the occasion."

Each napkin featured a young woman, peering through a magnifying glass. The message beside her read: "I don't like making plans for the day. Because then the word 'premeditated' can be thrown around in the courtroom."

Everyone burst into laughter.

Over dinner, I repeated most of what Chief Marshall had shared with me. Although the poison-by-flower-petals death surprised them, we all agreed Michael was the logical suspect.

Nellie passed the bread to Sharon. "I really liked the guy. From what Betty told us, he was super nice."

Sharon shook her head. "You didn't see him arguing with Thomas at the pickleball court. He was angry. Maybe angry enough to kill someone."

Kate set her wineglass on the table. "We saw Thomas the day after the pickleball incident. He said he was embarrassed by the whole exchange. Michael always complained about how Thomas ruined his chances with Betty by introducing her to Bob. But, this time, he seemed enraged by some harsh words Bob had said to Betty. Thomas couldn't convince Michael to share the details, but it was something about a dance performance Betty wanted to do in New York."

"I suppose it would have been difficult for her to adjust to the small-town life after they moved here." Sharon's wide blue eyes peeked at us over her water glass. "I know it was hard on Terry to move his law practice here after working so hard to build it in Chicago."

"Something still bothers me about Betty's decision to leave the city," I confessed. "It doesn't feel right to me. She was so talented, and apparently very competitive. She had the career she had worked hard to achieve. Why would she leave it?"

Sharon nodded at me. "There must be more to that story. Maybe Bob insisted that she quit the ballet because he wanted to distance her from Michael."

Kate raised her wineglass to her lips. "Or maybe it was a practical matter. It's expensive to live in the city. I don't know how much ballerinas make, but a marine's pension is about half of their active duty pay. Bob probably wasn't providing much of their income. Could they have been short on money?"

Nellie sighed. "Well, whatever. I was hoping for a happy ending to the love story. I wanted someone else to be the murderer, so Michael could be around to help Betty through her loss."

"You're such a romantic," Kate teased. "I knew Michael did it. He was the only one that made any sense."

I set my wine glass on the table. "You're right, Kate. The only thing I keep wondering about is why he won't admit he did it. He has confessed that he was capable of everything except the actual murder."

Nellie frowned and leaned both elbows on the table. "Maybe he had an accomplice. Could he have talked the marine into helping him? Or Betty herself?"

We all looked at her in stunned silence for several seconds. Finally, I shook my head in confusion. "Well, now you've given us something more to think about."

After everyone left, I put Moe outside while I packed our leftovers into containers and put them into the refrigerator. Two minutes later, I heard Moe barking. There was a huge crash that sounded as if my trash can overturned onto the sidewalk, and I raced to the door to see who was outside. I remembered the chief wanted me to keep my doors locked, but I couldn't very well leave Moe outside, alone and in danger.

I needn't have worried about a human intruder. The moment I opened the door, the musky pungent odor of skunk hit my nostrils, making me gag. "Oh, Moe. What have you done?"

He looked up at me with big, sad eyes. This wasn't the first time he had been sprayed by a skunk, but neither of us was happy about the situation. I mixed up my special recipe for "Skunk Odor Removal" and led poor Moe into the bathroom. The concoction was one I'd used before with some success. Before I discovered this simple formula, I'd tried all the household remedies others had recommended, but the tomato juice shampoo left Moe smelling like a stinky tomato.

There was no other way to accomplish the task, so I put on a pair of shorts and a T-shirt and stepped into the shower with my smelly dog. By the time I'd thoroughly scrubbed him with the hydrogen peroxide and baking soda mixture, we were both wet and exhausted. My bathroom was a mess, but the skunk smell had almost disappeared.

After drying his fur with my hair dryer, Moe turned in three weary circles before he collapsed onto his cozy dog bed. He was snoring loudly before I slipped into pajamas and turned out the light. My last thought was of Sharon. I couldn't wait to tell her about Moe's latest adventure.

Chapter Twenty

I didn't sleep well that night. The investigation felt like one of my grandmother's jigsaw puzzles with pieces in the wrong places. I knew something was missing, but I couldn't put it together. Harvey's questions replayed in my mind. I wanted desperately to get out of bed and write note cards for the various scenarios so I could sort through them. At 5 a.m., I gave up, put on my house slippers, and started a pot of coffee. Moe gave me a questioning look as he followed me into the kitchen.

"I know it's early, boy, but I can't sleep."

He tilted his head. If dogs could shrug their shoulders, he would have done that too. Instead, he ran outside to take care of his morning business. When he returned, I had my pack of note cards stacked and ready. Moe made himself comfortable under Grandma Molly's table. Within minutes, I filled twenty cards, and Moe snored softly at my feet.

I spent a couple of hours trying to connect the dots before I gave up. All I had was an empty coffee pot and a table filled with note cards. I couldn't seem to reconcile the discrepancies. Betty loved Bob. What could he possibly have said to make her turn on him? There was no way I could see her as an accomplice.

Why had the marine argued with Michael? Was there a festering issue between the two marine buddies? Could he have a hidden agenda?

There were simply too many unanswered questions to draw any conclusions. I made breakfast and set the note cards aside. My routine Monday errands were listed on the calendar affixed to my refrigerator door. They stared back at me, a stark reminder that dabbling in murder cases wasn't on the list. I decided to take care of my commitments before I spent any additional time thinking about Bob's murder. It wasn't my responsibility; the chief would agree.

Moe hopped into Piper's back seat and we drove through town with the top down. I caught a whiff of skunk odor when the breeze ruffled his coat, but I tried hard to ignore it. Fortunately, his appointment with the groomer was on today's errand list.

We stopped by the post office and mailed thank-you notes to several friends who had remembered my birthday a couple weeks earlier and pooled together to give me a spa day. Then, we drove through the teller window at the bank to make a deposit. Maryann asked me what I thought about Mr. Wilson's arrest, but I smiled and shook my head. "I'm glad it's over." She slipped a dog biscuit for Moe into my envelope.

I dropped my slightly smelly companion at the groomer's for a bath and trim before I headed to my mechanic's shop. Mr. Nutter's son, Lee, was expecting me for a scheduled oil change and a new windshield wiper blade. As I waited in his comfortable lounge, I checked emails on my cell phone. There was a group text from Sharon that made me smile: "We play mahjong at my house this Wednesday. I will *not* be serving pie, but I have another surprise for you to taste. Who's in?"

Quickly, I sent a reply: "I'll be there."

Wandering out into the repair shop, I chatted briefly with Lee as he worked. The murder was on his mind as well. "So, they arrested the botanist."

"That's what I heard," I said noncommittally.

"Do you really think he did it?"

"He's practically confessed to everything."

"But do you think he did it?"

"I don't know," I answered. "I can't seem to figure out anyone else with the motive *and* the opportunity Mr. Wilson had."

"Time will tell." Lee's voice drifted out from under the hood of my car.

"Did you know Mr. Hamilton?"

"Sure." His voice echoed across the concrete room. "I worked on his Jeep."

"What did you think of him?"

"It's hard to say." Lee walked around the car, wiping his hand on an oily red cloth he pulled from his pocket. "I have an opinion, but I'm not sure I can say it out loud in the presence of a lady."

"That bad?" I joked.

"He was more than a little picky about his Jeep. The man was hard to please."

"Hmm. He was nice when I was interviewing Betty."

"Mechanics don't always see the best of people. But that guy? He struck me as someone who was used to being in charge. I can see how there might be hard feelings between Mr. Hamilton and another man who had a past relationship with his wife."

At 11 a.m., I decided to stop by Lorene's Cozy Cups Cafe. The town was buzzing with the news, and I wondered what she had heard. This was a tricky subject, since Lorene was married to the chief, but who better to take the pulse of the community than the owner of our local coffee shop?

The little café smelled like hot coffee and fresh bread; my mouth was watering before I grabbed my favorite cup and headed for the coffee bar. Lorene was known for her wide assortment of mismatched cups and mugs. Customers selected one from the racks near the door and served themselves at the coffee bar. I squirted two pumps of vanilla bean syrup into my coffee and then swirled in a few drops of cream.

Lorene spotted me at the corner table and made a beeline to where I sat. "Mind if I join you?"

"I was hoping you would."

"Earl is all worked up about solving the case. He's got the whole town feeling upbeat about it, but he is stewing over the details."

"You know he likes to cross all the T's."

"Seems to me, this case was delivered to him all nice and tidy. Wrapped with a ribbon and bow."

"You're complaining because it was too easy?"

"We're not accustomed to 'easy' in our house."

Chapter Twenty-One

On my way to pick up Moe, I took a chance that the farmer's market might be open and drove a block out of my way to check. Only two stalls had vendors: Scott's Produce and Melanie's Melons. Their displays were creative and colorful, with vibrant produce that looked too delicious to ignore. A few customers remained, thumping melons and making their selections.

I parked on the street and walked toward them, waiting patiently for other customers to complete their purchases. Both vendors waved to acknowledge my arrival.

Melanie had combined wooden packing crates with bright red wheelbarrows to showcase her crops. She had sorted the melons by size and variety, and I marveled at her ingenious marketing skills. Deep green basketball-sized melons were stacked into a bright red wheelbarrow with a handwritten "Seedless Sugar Baby" sign, while the picnic-size "Crimson Sweet" watermelons were displayed in a larger wheelbarrow beside them. The wooden boxes were turned on their sides, with a variety of smaller produce spilling out of the boxes. There were honeydews, cantaloupes, butternut squash, and zucchini. It was a jumble of bright greens and yellows, with a few striped melons in between. Pete Scott's display was artfully arranged in the back of his faded blue pickup truck.

Melanie's customers dispersed first, and she welcomed me with a smile. "We knew the weekend would be packed with outsiders for the Summer's End Festival. So, we brought in plenty of melons." She waved her arm across three wheelbarrows and four additional crates overflowing with watermelon and cantaloupe. "We sold most of them, but these still need to go. I'll give you a deal on a dozen of each."

"There's only one of me. I'll take a couple of the Sugar Baby melons and one cantaloupe. I can share them with someone."

Turning to Pete Scott, I motioned to his sign offering the freshest tomatoes in town. "I came for tomatoes and cucumbers. What do you have left?"

He walked with me to the rear of his truck, where the tailgate was down, and bushel baskets of produce poured onto burlap bags in a colorful heap. There were several shades of cucumbers I didn't recognize.

"This one is a lemon cucumber." Pete sliced the round yellow ball like I would cut a pie and handed me a piece. "They are obviously named for their color and shape. They taste like a milder version of the traditional cucumber. There's nothing sour about them."

As he was bagging my order, I noticed a small shelf featuring home-canned goods at the side of the truck bed. Five pint-size jars stood in a row. Each had a simple label, neatly written in bold feminine handwriting: "Scott's Salsa."

The label looked familiar, and I recalled who had been talking about salsa recently: the chief had mentioned that Bob Hamilton's report showed traces of poison and *salsa*.

My heart raced a little at the realization that this might be the salsa Bob Hamilton was eating the day I interviewed Betty. I tried to speak calmly as I turned to Pete. "I didn't know you sold canned goods."

"That was a new addition this summer. My wife makes a mean salsa from our fresh tomatoes. You should try it."

"I'll take three jars. Can you tell me, was Bob Hamilton one of your customers?"

"Terrible thing about Bob, wasn't it? Yes, he loved our salsa. He bought it by the case."

"Don't you lease some land to them for planting?"

"Not from Mr. Hamilton," Pete said. "We had a couple of conflicts with him in the beginning, so we handled our lease through Betty."

"What kind of conflicts?"

Pete shrugged. "Nothing big. Mr. Hamilton wanted a percentage of our sales, and all we wanted to do was lease the land."

"Why do you think he wanted a percentage?"

"Probably so he could make more money, But Betty stepped in and worked it out. After Bob discovered our salsa, the disagreement was forgotten."

"Did anyone else ever buy it for him?"

"Sure did. That marine buddy of his, Thomas Fisher. And Betty, of course. And once or twice Betty's assistant picked some up. Alyssa Burney."

"What about Mr. Wilson?"

"Can't say that I know him. But I'll bet he would like it if he's a salsa guy."

"Thanks, Pete. I'll give it a try."

As he piled my produce and the salsa into a burlap bag and handed it to me, I noticed another small sign in the truck bed:

FRESH EGGS.

"You keep chickens at the farm?"

"Yeah. We ran out of eggs early, though. You're too late for those."

"Any chance you're missing some hens?"

Pete stared at me, his mouth open. "Why, yes, we are. We figured some kids stole them on a lark. Half a dozen of our hens and one chicken crate went missing Friday night. How'd you know?"

I shook my head. "Long story. The hens showed up on my back deck. Somebody's idea of a joke."

"I'm so sorry. I don't know anything about that. We didn't report the theft. We figured it might not be worth the effort. It's hard to identify a chicken."

"No problem. You can pick them up at the police station."

I'd barely loaded my purchases into the trunk of my little convertible and started down the road when my cell phone rang.

"This is Josie."

"Josie, it's me, Betty. Do you have time to talk?"

I pulled Piper to a stop under the shade of a huge walnut tree near the historic park and turned off the engine. "I'm on my way to pick up Moe at the groomer's. How are you doing?"

"I'm devastated." I could hear the tears in her voice. "I've lost Bob, and now they've arrested Michael."

"Have you talked to him?"

"He called yesterday. I'm trying to convince him to get an attorney. That's why I wanted to talk to you. Do you know any criminal lawyers you would recommend? I don't know where to begin. But I do know that he's innocent."

"Are you absolutely sure about that?"

"Positive. Michael could never harm anyone."

"He does get angry, though. My friend saw him arguing with Thomas at the pickleball court last week."

"Just because someone gets into an argument doesn't make them capable of murder," she insisted.

I agreed with her and promised to let her know if I thought of a good attorney. "I could give you the names of three corporate law firms, but criminal law is totally different."

"Please, Josie. I need your help. Michael didn't do this, and you must figure out who did. The chief isn't looking at anyone else now that he has Michael in custody."

I thought about her plea all the way to the groomer's. She sounded desperate and heartbroken. I couldn't imagine the pain she must be feeling, but I didn't have the resources she needed. In fact, I couldn't think of anyone in my circle of friends who would know a criminal attorney. Betty was right. The only way I could help her—and Michael—was to identify the real murderer.

For the ride back home, Moe hopped into Piper's back seat proudly, his fluffy coat blowing in the summer breeze. If Moe's jaunty attitude was any indication of the doggy mindset, I was sure dogs knew when they looked their best. As usual after his grooming, Moe expected a treat. We went directly to the ice cream shop, where the girl at the drive-through made a special doggy cup for Moe. I set the paper bowl on the floor. He jumped down and quickly ate the treat. Afterwards, he gave me a sloppy "thank you" kiss with a wet lick across the back of my head.

At home, we unloaded the car, and I returned to the note cards that were still spread across my table. There must be a solution to this murder that didn't point to Michael Wilson.

My determination to leave the case in Chief Marshall's capable hands was beginning to falter. What if the chief really needed my help? Why else would he have shared the details of the case?

As I pondered the cards, my phone rang again.

"This is Josie."

"Josie, this is Thomas." I would have recognized the marine's gruff voice, even without his introduction.

"What can I do for you, Thomas?"

"I wanted to talk to you about Michael Wilson."

"The last time we talked, you said you felt he was capable of murder."

"Yes, I did. I still think that. Anyone is capable of murder under the right circumstances."

"If you believe he did it, why are you calling me?"

"Because even though I know he could do it, I no longer think he did."

"And why is that?"

"Because I spoke with Michael yesterday, and he showed so much concern for Betty that I am now convinced he would not have killed her husband. He was genuinely distraught that anyone would take from Betty the one man she truly loved."

By the end of the afternoon, I had developed a headache. On the one hand, I didn't want to bother the chief again. On the other hand, I thought he needed to know about what I'd learned today. What if the poison that killed Bob had been mixed into salsa from the farmer's market? Was it in the salsa Betty offered me the first day we met? The chief would want to know who purchased it. And I had to tell him about the missing chickens.

Sighing, I picked up my phone again. But, before I could dial it, the phone rang. The caller ID surprised me: it was Chief Marshall.

Chapter Twenty-Two

I picked up the phone and answered, "Yes."

"Jo, I need you to come to the station. There's been a new development." The chief sounded excited on the other end of the line. He was making a habit of calling me into the case. Proof that my theories are valuable.

"I'm on my way," I said.

It was after five when I pulled into a parking spot at the police station. Chief Marshall called me into the familiar little conference room and closed the door behind us.

"Betty has found several notes that Bob had hidden around the house. I'd like you to join me there tonight, if you can."

"Okay." I wondered briefly why he wanted me there. "Are they written in a code or something?"

"Bob had a habit of slipping cryptic notes into hiding places where he knew Betty would find them. Some were notes of affection or encouragement, others were riddles. She's found a few in the last couple of days that she believes might be clues."

"And you want me to help figure them out?"

"Betty trusts you. Having you there will make her more comfortable. She may be more willing to share her thoughts."

"Sounds good. By the way, I found the owner of your chickens: Pete Scott."

"The same Pete who's on our suspect list?"

"He says they went missing Friday night. He hasn't had time to report it yet."

"I'll check it out."

We talked for a few minutes more, and the chief told me he still felt Michael was the most likely suspect.

"He's not admitting it, but I know there was a serious argument between him and the victim shortly before the murder. I think he's protecting someone. I can't get him to share details."

"Is he still here?"

"Yep. He didn't want an attorney, so he's still being detained. Do you want to talk to him?"

"I could go in as a visitor, to see how he's doing."

The chief walked me down the hall to one of only two confinement rooms our little police station offered. It didn't look much like a jail. There were no iron bars defining the space. Instead, there was a locked door with a good-sized window. The glass was laced with mesh, but I could easily look through it to see Michael Wilson sitting comfortably on a reclining chair. He was watching an episode of *Judge Judy* on the small television sitting on the desktop opposite him. A small cot, and a nightstand with a lamp, lined the back wall.

"That's not too bad, for a jail cell."

"It's our temporary holding cell. We're still getting the paperwork ready to file, so it seemed like the best place to keep him. He doesn't appear to be a danger to anyone else."

I knocked politely on the door and pressed the intercom button. "Hi, Michael. I'm Josephina Posey. Mind if I come in and chat?"

The botanist turned toward the window and gave me a smile and a wave. "Come on in. I've got nothing but time."

"I see you're studying the justice system," I motioned to the television set where Judge Judy was ruling on a case.

"Something like that. You never know what you will learn from a television program."

He offered me the chair and waited for me to sit. Then, he folded his six-foot frame in one flowing movement to settle onto the cot across from me. Immediately, I was struck by how attractive he was. I'd never officially met Michael and had seen him only briefly at the flower shop. Here, in this tiny room, his charismatic presence was undeniable. He had striking green eyes and one of those artistic faces that Michelangelo might have chiseled from marble. It was an interesting combination of high cheekbones and a square jaw that somehow made him appear both strong and intellectual. I could picture him in either profession: performing in front of an audience or peering into a microscope.

"I know we haven't met," I began, "but I've heard so much about you from Betty that it seems like I know you."

"She's a wonderful woman."

"Yes. I interviewed her for our local newspaper. Her background is impressive."

"You're a reporter?"

"Oh, no," I stammered. "Well, not today, anyway. I was a crime reporter in the city. Now, I write profiles on some of our town's interesting residents. That's not why I'm here to see you."

"So, I'm not interesting?" He raised one eyebrow and gave me a quizzical smile.

I laughed. "You definitely are. And to be honest, I will be writing a story about the murder, when it's solved. Right now, I'm here to learn more about you. I can see why Betty said you're a special person. She said you had a great sense of humor."

"We've been through a lot together. I don't think many people realize how much."

"Would you mind sharing some of that with me? I'd like to understand her better. I can't figure out why she left a promising career in New York to move here. And, I don't see how Thomas Fisher fits into the picture."

Michael sat quietly on the cot for a few moments. I waited without speaking.

"Ms. Posey."

"Please, call me Josie."

"Josie Posey?" He said my name slowly, a smile crossing his face.

"That's the name." I nodded ruefully. "It's a curse, but it's memorable."

122

"It certainly is. Well, Josie Posey, I'm a pretty good judge of character, and I can already tell you are a woman to be trusted. So, let me tell you a love story."

"Please do. But it must have a happy ending. I don't want to hear anything that will make me cry."

"It's happy."

For the next twenty minutes, Michael Wilson talked. He told me about how he met Betty in a college dance class and how he fell in love with her. He loved her beauty, her talent, and her dedication. Most of all, he loved her kind and gentle nature.

"Even as a college student, Betty saw everything through a lens of joy. It never crossed her mind that anyone would purposefully hurt someone else. She couldn't imagine it because she would never do it herself. But that made her vulnerable in a career filled with ambitious people vying for only a few principal dancer positions."

"But she had the talent to make it," I added.

"Yes. She made it, but she paid a heavy price, emotionally."

"I'm not sure I understand what you mean."

"Betty shared everything she had with the other ballerinas in the dance company. She taught them how to do the more difficult moves, such as how to hold an arabesque for a full two minutes and how to master the proper technique. But, the more she gave, the more her classmates resented her talent. She had only a few friends; they dropped off one by one, leaving her all alone at the pinnacle of her career."

"How did she deal with that?"

"Betty built a wall around herself and hid her insecurities. Until the one person she still trusted betrayed her."

"What happened?"

"Her roommate intercepted an updated practice schedule from the ballet director. As a result, Betty missed several sessions. The roommate took her place. She claimed that Betty relied on opioids to ease her muscle pain and was increasingly unreliable. The director believed the story."

"But it wasn't true."

"Like most good fabrications, the lie was rooted in an element of truth. Betty did have a prescription for oxycodone from a physician who treated her when she injured a tendon in her ankle. She never took the pills, but the bottle was in the top drawer of her nightstand – exactly where the roommate said it would be."

"How terrible."

"For Betty, it was unbearable. She had an emotional breakdown and spent six weeks recovering in a private psychiatric hospital for dancers and models. It's called The Clarus House."

"I had no idea mental health was such a big issue for professional dancers."

"Oh, yes. They struggle with depression, eating disorders, body dysmorphia, and general anxiety. If you visited The Clarus House today, you might find as many dancers in their facility as there are runway models and actresses."

I didn't like where this was leading. "You promised your story would have a happy ending."

"It does. Through that experience, Betty learned what she really enjoyed most was *teaching* ballet, not performing it. So, she chose to move far away from the big city and establish her own studio. She spends her time teaching children how to approach dance in a healthy way—including their mental health. She also goes back to New York to choreograph several performances connected to charities that raise money for mental health in the dance world."

"Was Bob supportive of those charity performances?" I asked.

"No. It was one of the things he and I argued about. Even my buddy Thomas didn't understand how important the benefit performances were to Betty. They kept her connected to the dance world, and they gave her a way to improve the lives of hundreds of dancers."

"Bob didn't want her to go?"

"Bob *forbade* her to go. He believed the trips drained her energy and threatened her emotional stability."

"Betty disagreed," I said as the picture became clearer.

"Betty disagreed, and I stood up for her. She had a right to make her own decisions. All I ever wanted was for her to be happy."

CHAPTER TWENTY-TWO

"Even when it came to marrying Bob?"

"I would have preferred that she marry me." Michael smiled as he thought of the woman he loved. "But, after she met Bob, I could see how much she loved him. When he walked into the room, she lit up."

"It wasn't that way with the two of you?" I pushed.

"Unfortunately, no. I loved her from the moment I saw her. But she couldn't see anyone but Bob. Once I realized that, I knew I'd spend the rest of my life in his shadow."

"Do you regret it?"

"I don't regret what I can't change," he answered. "The only alternative would have been to move far away, never seeing her again. I wasn't strong enough for that. It was better to have her as a friend than not to be around her at all."

It sounded romantic. It also sounded obsessive. Was there another alternative—a way to remove the one overshadowing his affections?

Chapter Twenty-Three

The chief had someone in his office as I left, so there was no time to talk to him about Betty's past or to share my list of salsa customers. That would have to wait until after we met at the ballerina's home that evening. My conversation with Michael made me realize he truly loved Betty and would do almost anything to be near her.

Still, something bothered me about the investigation. I was certain we were missing important details. As I drove past Miss Betty's School of Dance, I slowed the car and pulled to a stop directly in front of the building. For a moment, I closed my eyes and imagined the place filled with children in leotards while Betty stood at the front of the class, counting in time to the music: "One and two, three and four. Pirouette, two, three, four." In my mind, I could clearly see the little dancers intently following her instructions.

Feeling a little silly, I opened my eyes to find the building standing empty, as it was when I pulled into the parking spot. As I watched, the front door opened, and Alyssa came out, her bright pink dance bag slung over her shoulder. She turned to lock the door behind herself, and the swirl of her skirt turned this simple motion into a graceful dance move. I stepped out of my car to wait while she walked down the sidewalk toward me.

"Alyssa. How can you manage to juggle a dance bag and your keys and still spin as beautifully as a prima ballerina?"

Her lovely face lit up at my comment. "Well, it helps to be wearing ballet flats, but I doubt that you will find that twirl in any official dance choreography soon."

"You're working late again. Is everything okay?"

"I was finishing a paper for my dance theory class. It's due tomorrow."

"I didn't realize you had written assignments during the summer."

"Oh, yes. I was able to double up with my summer class by teaching here at the studio."

"So, you get class credit while you work?"

She nodded. "Betty arranged it. I had to combine my job with a research project, but it turned out to be a good way to accumulate some dance credits at the same time."

"What kind of research are you doing?"

"It's complicated. I'm studying the roles that body motion and sensorimotor experience play in the formation of concepts and abstract thinking."

"Whoa. That sounds challenging."

"It is." Her eyes lit up as she gave me a more detailed description. "It's theoretical right now, but some researchers believe dance/movements can be used as therapy. They are collecting evidence that dance can improve people's ability to think clearly. In some cases, it can even help people develop a more positive attitude that results in a generally improved sense of well-being."

"And you are contributing to this study?"

Alyssa looked startled. "Oh, no. I haven't paid any money toward the research," she said.

I smiled at her. "I meant through your own study. The report you are doing will impact the research results."

"Well, yes. But my part is really small." Alyssa ducked her head modestly. "I'm studying how dance impacts the sense of well-being in children. I began with a survey when the students first enrolled. I did a follow-up survey midway through the class and another at the end."

"It must feel good to have finished your paper."

"It does. I've worked hard on it."

"Do you mind if I ask how you happened to come here, to English Village?"

She shrugged her shoulders, and her eyes twinkled as she answered. "This has always been my home."

"You're from English Village?"

"Born and raised. My mom and dad enrolled me in dance classes here when I was in kindergarten. Of course, Betty wasn't here then. You might say I danced in this studio before she did."

"And now you're teaching children the same dance steps you learned as a little girl."

She nodded. "The choreography changes, but classical ballet movements have been the same forever."

"What's next for you? Will you be teaching at the studio during your fall semester?"

A brief shadow crossed her face. "We're trying to figure that out. Betty may decide to take some time off. I had hoped to do an internship with the ballet in New York or Chicago, but nothing has come through yet."

"Well, I'm sure you'll be dancing your way to a big stage somewhere soon. For now, it's nice to have your talent here in English Village."

We both backed out of our parking spots, and Alyssa gave me a friendly wave as she drove off. I turned Piper's satellite radio to "Sixties on Six" and sang along with an old Bobby Vinton song as I headed toward home. It was still a couple of hours before I needed to meet the chief at Betty's.

Moe sat by the door, leash in his mouth, when I turned my key in the lock. "Okay, boy," I told him. "Give me a minute, and we'll go for a walk."

Picking up my phone, I dialed Kate. "Want to join us for our daily walk?"

"Sure. I was about to take Bacon to the park. Meet you at the bench?"

I loved that Kate could be as spontaneous as I was. We often did this spur-of-the-moment dog walk together. Bacon and Moe enjoyed it as much as we did. Within minutes, we were at the meeting point and took the fork onto the broad walking path that circled the park.

"Last time we were here," Kate said, "we ran into the dog walker with those yapping terriers."

"Yes, and you interrogated him about the murder. What if he had killed Bob? You could have been in danger."

"Nah," Kate scoffed. "That guy couldn't kill anyone. He's a dog lover."

"You may be right. Anyway, the chief is now convinced that Michael killed the ballerina's husband. I'm going to Betty's house tonight to search them for clues. Apparently, Bob left notes hidden all around the house. Betty is going to show them to me."

"You're doing what?" Kate exclaimed. "Does the chief know?"

"He invited me. He thinks Betty will open up to me more than she would to him."

"That makes sense. Except I thought he didn't want you to get involved."

"I know the chief said he didn't want my help, but secretly, he likes the way my overly curious mind works."

"Is that so?" Kate raised an eyebrow.

"Absolutely. I take all of the facts that I learn from him, match them up with the details you and the other mavens provide, and...wah-lah!"

"Wah-lah?"

"You know what I mean. It's like magic. The solutions appear, seemingly from nowhere."

"Yes," she said soothingly. "I understand the meaning. Technically, the word is *voilà*."

I grinned at her. "Are you lecturing me?"

"Not at all. But I'm not sure the chief would describe the process in the way you do."

"Probably not. He isn't really a wah-lah kind of guy."

"But he appreciates your help, all the same," Kate assured me.

We circled the remainder of the park, passing by the blacksmith shop as we neared our original starting point. Kate motioned toward the door. "Want to stop in and say hi to Harvey?" She gave me an innocent look.

"You're impossible."

"Seriously. He's a great guy, and I can tell he likes you. Plus, he makes beautiful iron art."

"I like him too. But I don't think I'm ready to consider dating."

"Don't be so sure. You never know. You could have a wah-lah moment. Keep an open mind."

I rolled my eyes at her.

Chapter Twenty-Four

The chief and I stood together on Betty Hamilton's front porch and rang the doorbell. Wind chimes tinkled softly beside us, and I noticed a lovely piece of hand-tiled artwork hanging to the side of the doorbell. It was an abstract ballerina, beautifully crafted from luminous jewel-tone ceramic tiles. I wondered why I hadn't noticed it earlier.

Betty opened the door wide, inviting us in. I took the moment to learn more about the artwork. "Is this ballerina a new addition?"

"Yes, and no. Michael gave it to me a few years ago when he returned from a trip to Spain. I've kept it in the box until now but decided to hang it today."

"It's lovely."

"Honestly, Bob never cared for it. I think it was one of those small things he resented about Michael—his way of discovering little gifts that I adored. But now, it seems important that I hang it for everyone to see. Bob is gone, so it won't be hurtful to him. And Michael could use a show of support."

"That makes sense."

She spoke so calmly about the strained relationship between the two men that I wondered if she had forgotten that we were here to discuss Bob's murder. I watched her for telltale signs of nervousness, but there were none.

Chief Marshall listened to the exchange without commenting. Then we followed her into the sunroom at the rear of the house. Betty stood near the table where I had interviewed her a few days ago. "Before I show you what I found, I would like to provide some background information."

"I'd appreciate that," I said. "The chief may already know some of this, but I'd like to hear anything you think might be helpful."

We took a seat around the table, and then Betty clasped her hands. "Bob was a military man in every sense of that description," she began. "He was organized and structured. Punctual to a fault. He lived a life of black and white. He had no patience for anything in-between. For him, things were right or wrong. I loved that he could focus on a goal and head directly toward it, without distractions."

"Are you saying he was rigid and inflexible?" I asked.

Betty shook her head. "He was a man who knew what he wanted, and he tried his best to get it. He wasn't perfect, of course. No one is. But he came very close."

"Is that why you fell in love with him?" I prodded.

"Partly." Her eyes misted as she described how they met. "It was at a charity ball. He was in his United States Marine Corps dress blues, with medals in tight rows that filled his entire left breast panel. But I noticed him because he stood apart from the others. He seemed to be the calm one, unaware of the bustling noise around him. I liked that he was in control, without appearing to notice everyone deferring to him."

"Did you normally date military types?"

"Never," Betty answered with a short laugh. "I was a dancer. Everyone I met was an artist or a performer. We were disciplined, in our way, but none of us ever felt in control of our own destiny. The men I dated were focused on themselves. But Bob looked directly into my eyes from across that room, and I knew he would care for me and protect me from the world."

The chief looked at me to continue the conversation. He shrugged his shoulders as if to say, "You started this, Josie; now, keep her talking."

I thought for a moment before I continued. "Was there...a downside to your relationship?"

"When we first met, I was in a fragile state of mind," Betty said. "I was at the peak of my career, but I wasn't confident, emotionally. Bob took charge. Simply standing beside him made me feel stronger."

"But?"

"But he wasn't good at communicating his feelings. So, there came a time when we had to figure out how to have a real relationship. We had to learn how to talk with each other and share our thoughts."

"And how did you do that?"

"I proposed that we try something I learned in therapy: writing notes to each other. I explained to my husband that, while I loved feeling protected, I still needed my independence. Otherwise, our relationship would become too confining, and I would begin to resent his dominance."

Betty stood and walked across the room to pick up a small snow globe. She carried it to the chief and placed it in his hands. "I gave this to Bob the day we decided to try our therapy process. I shook the globe until the snow swirled in a blizzard around the little golden bird inside. I told him we needed to find a way to calm the storm so the bird could understand her place in the world. He agreed to try."

The chief handed the glass globe back to her. "Have you written notes to each other every day since then?"

"Not every day, but at least several times a week. We began by leaving the notes in a glass bowl. Mine were on pink slips of paper, and his were white. We would each pull out a note from the other and read it aloud. Then, we would talk about what the message meant to us. Later, we no longer needed the notes as a prompt to share our feelings."

I shook my head in wonder. "What a simple system. It fit within Bob's comfort zone of a structured program but allowed you both to discuss important emotions."

"Yes. I think it saved our marriage."

"But you were still writing notes, even after you grew much closer?"

"The funny thing was, Bob came to enjoy leaving notes in places where he thought I might be surprised to find them. It was his way of being spontaneous, and of expressing his feelings. Sometimes the notes would simply say 'I love you,' but other times they were conversation starters or puzzles."

"Betty, can you tell us about the notes you've found since Bob's death?" the chief interjected.

"I've left the three notes exactly where I found them. I hope you can help me figure out what he was trying to tell me."

We walked together into their bedroom, where Betty opened a small music box centered on her dresser. "Bob gave me this ballerina music box on our first date. I listen to it often, so he knew I would find a note hidden here."

We came closer and bent toward the handwritten note:

> *Always remember that admiration and jealousy*
> *are two sides of the same coin.*

Next, she guided us to her walk-in closet, where she had taken a shoebox from the shelf and set it on a decorative cushioned bench. She opened the box lid to reveal a pair of pink satin pointe shoes with long silk ribbons.

"I wore these shoes in my last performance. Bob knew I planned to go to New York to perform another charity event this fall. He probably expected me to discover the note there."

Again, we bent our heads closer to read the note:

> *No bond is stronger than the one between*
> *a brother and his sister.*

Finally, we followed Betty to a small potting shed outside the sunroom attached to the side of the house. "Bob loved to take care of our flower gardens. He spent a lot of time working on them—keeping them orderly and well-maintained. I sometimes joined him here, putting plants into big patio pots or arranging flowers into vases."

She opened a side cabinet filled with potting tools and then motioned toward the floral print gardening gloves hanging there. "He left this note inside the right glove." Bob's familiar handwriting stood out on the pale note that lay against the butcher-block workspace:

> *I don't subscribe to Sir Robert Walpole's*
> *famous saying.*

Betty had Googled Walpole to discover that, as the first prime minister of

Great Britain, Walpole was most famous for saying "Let sleeping dogs lie."

It doesn't happen often, but I was speechless. This clue might be the most confusing of all. I turned to the chief. We carried the notes back into the sunroom, where he peered closely at each one, as puzzled as I was.

"Do you have any idea what they mean?" The chief looked back at Betty.

"I've been trying to guess. They could be nothing. Bob sometimes left messages to spark a conversation about the topic. Once, we spent an entire afternoon discussing a cryptic quotation he had discovered on a tombstone in the little cemetery by the church."

Finally, I found my voice. "But you think these are somehow related to his murder?"

Betty lowered herself gracefully onto the sofa. "I believe the clues are related to a premonition. Bob was quite intuitive. If he had known someone planned to kill him, he would have taken a more direct action—like calling you, Chief. But if he only had a vague feeling something wasn't right, he would have written notes like these so we could talk about his apprehensions."

The three of us talked for a while about what the notes might mean but failed to come to any conclusions. In the end, we agreed to several points:

First, the reference to "admiration and jealousy" could refer to someone jealous of either Betty *or* Bob. Next, the reference to the "brother and sister" relationship could refer to Betty's relationship to Michael. And, finally, the reference to Sir Walpole's quote might be about leaving an old grudge unspoken or a problem unresolved—something Bob apparently didn't endorse

We ended the visit with more questions than answers. I drove home as confused as ever.

Chapter Twenty-Five

I felt Moe's hot breath on my face and squeezed my eyes closed. I wasn't ready to wake up yet. Not to be deterred, he rested his head more firmly on the bed. This was one of his favorite tactics. He stayed nose-to-nose with me, watching and waiting, until I gave up and opened my eyes. Then, he ran in happy circles around the bedroom until I surrendered and climbed out of bed. It was hard to ignore a 100-pound Old English sheepdog when he wanted attention.

While Moe did a morning romp in the backyard, I turned on the coffee and toasted a bagel. My list for the day was already on the kitchen counter, where I had left it around midnight. This late-night list-making habit was one I developed in my college days.

During the night, I slept fitfully, flitting from dream to dream. In one brief episode, I untangled Moe's leash from the dog walker's terriers; in another, I saw Michael calmly sitting on a witness stand as the judge proclaimed him guilty. The most disturbing dream involved little ballerinas in pink tutus. They danced in front of a mirror until the music stopped, and they all stood still, turning to Miss Betty for direction. But Betty wasn't there; Alyssa had taken her place. I thought her research into how dance might improve cognitive abilities sounded fascinating. The young dancer might be at the forefront of developing some interesting theories. I tried again to visualize Alyssa with Larry, but the two of them seemed to have nothing in common.

The sun painted broad streaks of crimson across the sky as I opened the door to let Moe back inside. It was barely dawn, and I had a full day ahead. Nellie and I were volunteering at the library today. After that, I was scheduled to pick up my new assignment from the newspaper—that is, if Leslie still wanted me to do a weekly profile of someone in our little village. Then, the chief and I were meeting at two to compare notes on the murder investigation.

Coffee steaming beside me, I sorted my note cards into neat rows on the big dining room table. I wrote additional cards to add to the piles. For nearly an hour, I scribbled names and hypothesized on potential meanings for the three notes Bob had left for Betty. I wondered what prompted him to leave those messages and whether there was any rhyme or reason to the locations of the notes.

Although no single solution jumped out at me, by the time I left for the library, I sensed some connections. I knew the links between Bob's notes and my narrowed list of suspects were incomplete, but I was sure they had potential. Like a faded old photograph in my grandmother's album, the solution seemed barely out of focus. I could see parts of the picture, but the details were too blurred to recognize. Perhaps stepping away from my obsessive stacks of cards for a while would clear my mind again.

Nellie arrived at the library before I did and was already at work, returning books to their proper places. "How's the investigation going?" she asked.

"I think we're close," I said optimistically. "I made another list."

"You and your lists. They're your secret to crime-solving."

"Either that, or they are my way of staying sane in the process. I'm going to call Betty during our break. Maybe she can help me with a few questions. That would make the list a little shorter."

"Is there anything I can do to help?" Nellie paused from shelving the books.

"I want to know a little more about Alyssa," I said. "She adores Betty, but I'm not sure how she felt about Bob. There's something nagging me about her."

"Wait till you hear what Kate told me this morning."

"What's that?"

"Kate said she and Faith—you know her mom, right? —saw Alyssa loading her car with luggage in the parking lot behind the dance studio."

"That doesn't seem unusual. She planned to head back to college for the fall semester soon."

"The packing wasn't unusual. But the guy helping her was a surprise. It was Larry, the dog walker. They were filling the trunk and yelling at each other." Nellie gave me a triumphant look.

"Funny." I stared at Nellie. "Especially after you and I saw them arguing in the alley by the bank on Saturday."

"Two arguments in two days. They must have a relationship of some sort," Nellie said.

"Maybe when Larry was hanging around the studio at the end of the day, he wasn't trying to catch a glimpse of Betty. He was waiting for Alyssa."

My friend shook her head. "I can't imagine her dating him. He's a bit of a hothead, still trying to figure out his future. She's a beautiful young girl with a lot of talent."

"You're right about that. Did you know she's taking a class on dance theory and how dance movements could be used as a therapy tool? Alyssa is more intelligent and focused than I realized. She has a serious side I hadn't seen before." I thought for a moment. "Maybe opposites attract?"

"If they are dating, Betty will know," Nellie said. "Add that question to your list."

We finished restocking the rolling cases of books, and I headed over to the children's area for Story Hour. About twenty young readers were gathered, waiting for me to read them a story. I settled into the rocking chair in front of them, but my mind was miles away, wondering about Alyssa.

Chapter Twenty-Six

I left the cool quiet of the library around noon. The sweltering heat of Kansas in late August hit me like a blast furnace as I hurried down the front steps and to my waiting car. It was far too hot to keep the top down on the little convertible; I cranked up the air conditioning and waited a moment for the interior to reach a reasonable temperature.

I wanted to ask the mavens for help figuring out Alyssa's behavior. But, first, a call to Betty might clear things up. The steering wheel was too hot to touch, so I stood outside in the shade while I made the call.

She sounded a bit breathless as she answered. "Hello."

"It's Josie. Did I interrupt you?"

"No, no. I was sorting through some papers. I have a stack of mail to get through and a couple of referral letters to send out."

"Actually, that's one of the questions I had for you. I spoke to Alyssa yesterday, and she mentioned she was hoping for an internship with one of the ballet companies. I wondered if you had given her a reference?"

I heard Betty hesitate on the other end of the phone. "I have one of those right here. I'm afraid I haven't been of much help to her—at least not in the way she wanted."

"Don't you want to support her?"

"Of course, I do. She's a talented young dancer, and I'd like to see her succeed."

"But?"

"Alyssa wants to start her career with a major ballet company. She's applying for internships in New York City, San Francisco, and Chicago.

138

I felt she should go into a smaller market first. She's very bright, but she's also a bit immature."

"Why wouldn't she aim for the top?"

"She could, but I worried that the competition in those companies would be too intense for her. Ballet can be viewed as a joyous pursuit of art, or it can be seen as a business. The bigger the reputation of the ballet company, the greater the chance that it is all about business."

"And you are afraid it could destroy her spirit?"

"Something like that. I know what it did to me, and I don't want to see that happen to Alyssa. She was disappointed, naturally. She thought I didn't believe in her talent."

"Did you agree to sign her referral letters?"

"Not until recently. I tried to convince her to slow down. I wanted her to start in a smaller environment—somewhere more nurturing. She insisted she wanted to go somewhere big. She's far more competitive than you might think."

"I heard about her dance theory research. It sounds complicated."

"Yes. Alyssa devotes all her energy to two things: learning about dance and becoming a better dancer. Sometimes she misses the bigger picture. She's still quite naive. She was upset with me for delaying her internship applications."

"I can see why."

"So can I, now. I was remembering my own struggles and assuming that Alyssa would experience the same things. That wasn't fair to her."

"No. It would be hard for Alyssa to understand your reluctance, even though you had her best interests at heart."

"After Bob died, I realized that I couldn't make decisions for Alyssa. She has a right to choose her own path. Now, I'm finally replying to a few of the requests. Unfortunately, I've caused her to miss some of the deadlines. I'm sure she isn't happy about that."

"She will have many more opportunities in the future."

"Yes. She's young, and youth never wants to wait on the future."

"Betty, I have two more questions about Alyssa."

"What are they?"

"First, how did she feel about Bob?"

Betty chuckled. "Alyssa really liked my husband. He was like a father figure to her. Did you know her own father abandoned their family?"

"No, I wasn't aware of that. Alyssa told me her parents enrolled her in dance lessons when she was young. I assumed she had a happy childhood."

"I believe she did," Betty added. "She was adopted by a wonderful couple who adored her. But her early memories of abandonment never quite went away. Alyssa still feels insecure at times."

"I'm surprised. She seems poised for her age. What made her feel close to Bob?"

"Bob didn't form close connections with many people, but he had a sweet spot for Alyssa. He always encouraged her. He told her that, except for me, she was the most beautiful dancer he had ever seen. Alyssa rewarded him with home-baked brownies. She knew he had a weakness for chocolate."

"Chocolate and salsa."

"Yes. An odd combination, but he loved them both. What is your last question?"

"Do you know whether Alyssa was dating anyone?"

"Not that I'm aware of. She seemed totally focused on her dance education, and on helping me with the studio. I never saw her with a young man."

"Someone told me she might be dating Larry Fox."

Betty's laugh was musical over the phone. "I seriously doubt it. Larry sometimes cleaned our building and took out the trash—that kind of thing. But I can't see Alyssa going out with him. From what I saw, he wasn't particularly interested in the things she cared about."

"Well, he sat in one of the front rows for the ballet performance at the Summer's End Festival. He must have had some reason to be there."

"I don't know. After he and Bob had their misunderstanding over the dogs and our flowerbeds, we didn't see much of him again."

I made a note of her comments and ended the call. It was time to head toward the newspaper office to pick up my next assignment.

The tiny editorial office could only be described as organized clutter. It was everything I had come to expect for a small-town newspaper. A little bell rang overhead when I pushed the glass door open, and five heads popped up to see who was entering. Two of them gave me a glance and then dropped their eyes back to their computer screens; they were pounding away against this week's deadline.

Two part-time clerks nodded at me over their ringing phones; they stayed at their desks, efficiently handling calls for classified ad information and obituary notices, lost pets, and news tips. Only the editor stood to meet me at the long counter that separated the public from the newsroom. Leslie Anderson had intelligent blue eyes behind practical wire-rimmed glasses. Her short blond hair was always a little messy—she had a habit of rubbing her scalp with her fingers when she bent over her desk to proofread the newspaper's pages. The woman was a whirlwind of energy. I never saw her without marveling over her ability to juggle multiple tasks simultaneously. She grabbed her coffee cup and a notepad, bringing them with her to the counter.

"How are you doing on the in-depth story of the murder investigation?" My editor wasted no time on small talk.

"I hope to meet this week's deadline."

"As you know, we postponed using your feature piece on Betty Hamilton. Now I've got a big hole to fill."

"I'm working on it." I assured her the case was nearly solved. I hoped that was true.

Leslie laid an assignment sheet on the counter in front of me. "We want to follow the murder story with an updated feature on Betty. With the news of her husband's murder still buzzing all over town, people will want to read about her."

"I'll have it ready in two weeks," I promised.

"Meanwhile, are you ready for a new assignment?"

"Sure. Who did you have in mind?"

Leslie smiled. "I wanted to do a story on Harvey Jacobs, but he asked that we wait until he could get the hardware store restocked for fall. He does some great iron art we could feature."

"I know. I've seen his work."

"See if you can talk him into an interview," Leslie said.

She handed me the paper with Harvey's contact information. I didn't mention that I already knew his number. Tucking the note into my purse, I turned to go back into the bright sunshine. First, I needed to wrap up a murder case.

Chapter Twenty-Seven

I had a couple of hours before my meeting with the chief, so I drove home to check on Moe. Nellie called as I pulled Piper into my driveway. "Do you have time for a chat?" Nellie wasn't one for idle conversations, so when she requested a meeting, I knew she had something specific on her mind.

"Always. Can you meet me at Cozy Cups around one? I'm going to the police station at two, but I have time for coffee and a sandwich. I'd also like to ask you another question related to the murder investigation."

"Perfect. I want your opinion on a new project too. I'll give you a quick summary, and we can talk more about it later.

I ran into the cottage to check on my sweet dog. Normally, he greeted me at the door, but today, I found him dozing inside the walk-in shower of my bathroom. This was one of his favorite spots in the heat of the summer. I refilled his water bowl and shooed him out the back door. While he was outside, I glanced through my mail and ran a comb through my hair.

Moe spent only a few minutes in the shady backyard before he was ready to return to our air-conditioned cottage. He was far too smart to waste time and energy chasing squirrels in 100-degree heat. I gave him a treat and promised I'd be home early, but he was already napping on the cool tile of the kitchen floor by the time I locked the door behind me.

Nellie arrived at the café ahead of me and was waiting at the self-serve coffee station. I could see she was excited about her latest idea. "What's up?" I asked.

"You're not going to believe this. We have an opportunity to bring a huge new event to English Village."

Lorene interrupted to bring us menus, but I waved them away. "I already have my coffee. I'd like an egg salad on rye. It's my favorite."

Nellie ordered a sugar-free muffin and a fruit plate. "I'm cutting back."

"You're always cutting back. If you cut back too much more, there won't be anything left of you. Tell me about this big event."

She leaned toward me eagerly. "It's an international juried art show, and they want to hold it *here*—in English Village."

"Wow. That does sound big. You're talking about selecting a jury of paid judges to curate the art before the show. Is it something we can handle?"

"With the right sponsors, I think we can make it happen." She went on to explain that she had reached out to the Hank English estate in London to suggest an event honoring him. "I told them we would like to do something special to expand on the art scholarships and workshops we do each fall."

"Adding a few more workshops is simple...but a juried art show is a lot of work, especially if you attract artists from around the world. They'll have to ship the art here. This is a big deal."

"I know. When I contacted them, I hoped they might send someone over to present the scholarships this year. Then, we could do a story in the newspaper and make it more of a tribute to our town's namesake."

"And they wanted more? Why am I not surprised when your ideas get bigger than you plan?"

"This one wasn't my idea," Nellie explained. "When I talked to his granddaughter, she said the family had been exploring the possibility of an art show to honor him. One thing led to another, and suddenly they were all excited about hosting it here in English Village."

"When do they want to do it?"

"Now." Nellie looked at me across the table, breathless. "We have two months to put it together. They want to start with a small show this year and then make it a major event next year."

"Oh, Nellie. This could be a disaster."

"Or it could be fantastic," she countered. "Will you help?"

Her infectious enthusiasm trumped my skepticism. "I'm in. Let's get a small group together and see what we can do. How about meeting this weekend?"

"I'll book the library conference room. We can outline our committees and have the plan ready to go by the end of the night."

"We'll have to get started if you want artists to submit their work in a month. Jurors will need a few weeks to do the judging, and we'll have to figure out exhibit space and prizes."

"They're giving us $50,000 to fund the project."

"Well, why didn't you say so? That will go a long way toward ensuring a successful event."

"You need to wrap up your murder investigation so we can work on the art show."

I reminded her it wasn't "my investigation" to complete. "The chief is getting close to solving it. We only have a few loose ends."

"Anything I can do?"

"Maybe." I hesitated. "What do you know about Alyssa Burney or Larry Fox? Kate said she saw them arguing yesterday, and no one seems to know they were dating."

"I don't know either of them that well. Do you really think they are dating?"

"It's just a theory."

Nellie thought for a moment before she pulled out her phone. "The one you need to talk to is Sharon. I'm sure she told me Alyssa was one of her second-grade students."

"Let's call her."

We asked Lorene to hold our order while we stepped outside to make the call. Nellie put our friend on speaker mode so we could both hear her response. I asked her the burning question:

"Do you know if Alyssa might be dating Larry Fox?"

Sharon laughed so hard I could picture her, head leaned back and eyes twinkling. "That's some theory."

"You think we're off track?" Nellie asked.

"Way off. Those two have always fought like cats and dogs. But I'm positive they aren't dating."

"You know them?"

"I've known them both since they were in grade school."

"I thought Larry moved here last spring."

"He did. But, when I was teaching, he was seven years old and in my second-grade class. His mom and her new husband introduced him to his new little sister, Alyssa, and he threw a fit about it. He was used to being the only child, and he wasn't crazy about a new baby girl in the house."

"Larry is Alyssa's brother?"

"Yes. After he got used to having a sister, the two of them became quite close. Alyssa's dad walked out before she was old enough for preschool. The mom fell apart, and both kids went into foster care."

"That's terrible. Did they split them apart?"

"They did. Alyssa ended up being adopted by a couple who doted on her. They took her everywhere and started her in ballet lessons as a child. Larry didn't fare as well. He moved from foster home to foster home. I think he was finally adopted when he was fifteen. Still, he managed to stay connected to her, and even tried to take care of her from a distance."

"What do you mean?"

"I remember he gave a kid a black eye in middle school because the boy tried to kiss Alyssa behind the gym. There was nothing he wouldn't do for his little sister, even after his foster family moved him to another town. He was away for at least ten years; he moved back here to support her as she started to attend college."

"Sharon, why didn't you tell me they were related earlier?"

"You never asked."

"You and Nellie know everyone—and *everything* about them."

"Not really," Nellie said. "I didn't know Alyssa was Larry's sister. I don't know who killed Bob. I don't even know where Lorene got the idea for the Cozy Cups Café."

"Let's ask her." We ended our call and went back inside to finish lunch.

When Lorene brought our checks, I raised Nellie's question. "Lorene, we've been wondering what made you decide to buy mismatched cups and name your entire café after them?"

Lorene gave us a wink. "Money. I didn't have any."

146

"What are you talking about?" Nellie motioned to the well-appointed cafe, with its stainless-steel kitchen and comfortable seating.

"I put so much into our kitchen that I ran short on our remodeling budget when it was time to stock up on tableware. So, I went to a bunch of garage sales and bought mismatched cups to have enough on hand for our opening day. We decided to name the café Cozy Cups and pretend it was all part of the plan."

"How did the chief react to that?"

"He grumbled, but soon he was shopping at all the garage sales with me. One weekend, we hit more than fifty sales, buying every coffee cup and teacup we could find. My husband turned it into a contest. Between us, we accumulated twelve dozen cups."

"Who won the contest?"

"Unfortunately, he did. Now he claims the mixed-up cups were all his idea."

I was still smiling about that story when I went to see the chief.

Chapter Twenty-Eight

"Did you get a good night's rest?" I already knew the answer from the dark circles under the chief's eyes.

"Not a wink. I was up late, catching a chicken thief. Then, when I finally went to bed, I tossed and turned until Lorene got up and made me a fresh pot of coffee early this morning."

"You caught the chicken thief?"

"Wasn't that difficult since he was right under my nose. Officer Devon mentioned to his twelve-year-old son that I referred to you and your friends as 'biddies.' He thought it was funny. Thought it might be a nice joke, using chickens to get you to back away from our case."

"It wasn't funny."

"No. The boy is grounded, and Devon is on a three-day suspension for the role he played in the Biddie Caper."

"The stunt has a name?"

"Thought you might enjoy that. You reporters are always looking for catchy headlines."

"Now that's funny."

"I'm sorry to have caused such an uproar, Josie. It was insensitive of me. If it's any consolation, I've lost a lot of sleep over this caper."

"You know, you need some rest. Sleep can be a powerful creativity booster."

"Is that right?" He sighed, waiting for the lecture he knew I was about to give him.

"It's true. The mind in an unconscious resting state can make surprising new connections that it perhaps wouldn't have made while we are awake.

In fact, a University of California at Berkeley study found that sleep could foster 'remote associates,' or unusual connections, in the brain—which could lead to a major aha moment upon waking. People are then 33 percent more likely to make connections between seemingly distantly related ideas."

The chief stared at me, finally comprehending what I was saying. "Have you figured out what we were missing?" Excitement played around the edge of his voice.

I grinned at him. "I believe I have. I might not have the final answer, but I have narrowed it down to two clear options."

Taking a marker from the rack below his whiteboard, I began to draw the timeline for Bob's murder. "See what you think of this theory."

In a column to the left side of the whiteboard, I made a list. "Whoever killed Bob had to know these things."

- **Naked Lady flowers are poisonous.**
- **Bob loved salsa.**
- **Betty never ate tomatoes, or salsa.**

"Yes." The chief nodded his agreement. "The killer not only needed to know these things, he or she needed to have access to them."

Next, I drew a large circle in the center of the whiteboard. I wrote Bob's name in the middle of the circle and wrote our suspects' names around the outside ring: Michael Wilson, Thomas Fisher*, Pete Scott*, Larry Fox, and Alyssa Burney*. "All of these people knew Bob or Betty, and most of them had reasons to be upset with Bob. To be fair, we have to include Betty in the suspect ring. She fits the profile too."

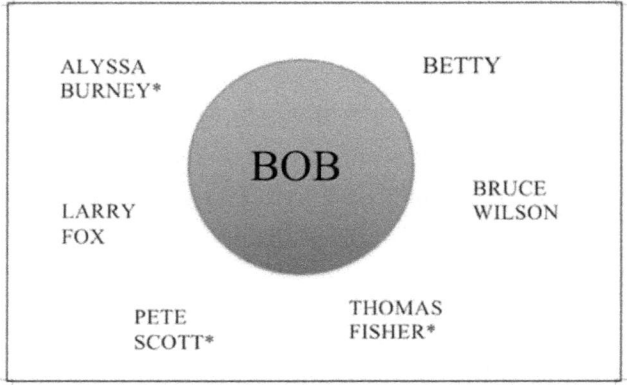

"The wife is always a suspect when a man is murdered. But, why the asterisks after the three names?"

"Those are the three people—besides Betty and Bob—who purchased the salsa or gave it to Bob. Pete Scott's wife made it this year for the market."

"We don't know of any animosity between Pete and the Hamiltons, do we?"

"No, but he fits all the other criteria. Pete was aware Bob loved salsa. He knew Betty didn't eat tomatoes because she never bought them. Since he is a gardener, we can probably assume he would know the Amaryllis belladonna flowers were poisonous."

"And the poison was in Pete's salsa. So, Pete could have a motive we haven't identified yet."

"Correct. That's why I left him on the list."

"And the marine?"

"He argued with Michael in public, so we know he had a temper. He also bought the salsa. We can assume he knew Betty didn't eat it. However, I'm still not sure he would choose poison as a weapon if he wanted to commit murder."

"What else have you been considering?"

"I believe we may have two murderers," I declared.

The chief listened intently as I gave my explanation: "Yesterday, when I talked with Michael in his cell, it occurred to me we had been looking for only one murderer. Michael seemed too calm to be guilty. It was almost as though he was doing something noble by admitting he could have killed the ballerina's husband. He came across like a hero."

The chief shook his head. "I've seen a lot of guilty people who appeared innocent."

"Yes, but something about that conversation made me think Bob's death could have involved two people—one with a motive and the other with the opportunity to administer the poison. Or, one to do the murder and the other to take the blame."

"That's an interesting theory." The chief massaged his temples. "It makes this investigation more complicated, but it could also explain why Michael hasn't actually admitted to killing Bob."

"Right. Maybe Michael had the motive, but Pete gave Bob the poisoned salsa."

"Or," the chief interrupted, "Michael and Betty shared a motive, but Betty gave Bob the poisoned salsa. Michael could be protecting her."

The chief pondered the board for several minutes before he turned to me again. "You said you narrowed the options to two possibilities. How do we cross some of these suspects off our list?"

"This is the part I'm not sure of," I admitted. "I may be connecting dots that don't exist. See what you think."

Taking the marker again, I made a new list on the far right of the whiteboard. This time, I wrote the clues we had deciphered from Bob's notes to Betty:

- **Admiration and Jealousy**
- **Brother and Sister**
- **Let sleeping dogs lie.**

Under each of these, I jotted the suspect names and a connection that seemed to match the clue. "For Admiration and Jealousy, the connections are easy to see."

"First, Michael Wilson admired Betty and was jealous of Bob; he's a prime suspect for that reason."

The chief grunted his agreement.

"Then, there's Betty Hamilton. She admired Michael and lived with Bob's jealousy. If Bob was increasingly controlling her, she might have been driven to kill him herself."

The chief nodded.

"And, finally, in this category, I put Alyssa Burney. She admired Betty but was jealous of her career."

"Yes, but surely that's not a reason to kill Betty's husband?"

"Maybe not," I conceded. "But this is only one category. Wait until you see the rest." I walked to the whiteboard again and began to make notes under the "Brother and Sister" category.

"Here, our list is limited. We have Michael Wilson and Betty Hamilton again. They shared what could be described as a brother-sister relationship, even though they were not related."

"I agree." Chief Marshall rubbed his chin. "And Bob's clue raised the point that 'no bond is stronger' than one between a brother and a sister. He may have been telling us Michael and Betty were closer than anyone knew. But, if that were the case, would Betty have shared that note?"

"It's doubtful. And today, I realized we have another brother-sister relationship to add to the list."

"Who? Is Thomas Fisher related to someone? Or Pete Scott?"

Carefully, I wrote the two additional names onto the board. "Larry Fox is Alyssa Burney's half-brother. And Nellie Nester told me Larry has always watched over Alyssa."

Chief Marshall scribbled some notes on the pad in front of him. "And here I thought we had ruled out Larry. The guy was pretty convincing when he said he would never murder anyone over a bad review of his business."

"That may be true. But would he kill someone who hurt his little sister?"

The chief paused before he spoke. "I think we need to look carefully at all the details before we jump to conclusions. What's next on your list?"

I walked to the whiteboard again to write under the third category. "Here's where the picture gets muddy. When Bob declared he didn't believe in letting 'sleeping dogs lie,' he may have been telling us he was ready to confront the past. Over the years, Bob and Michael Wilson had an unspoken agreement to leave things as they were. They didn't dwell on the past or talk about their shared love of one woman—"

Chief Marshall interrupted, "So, the two of them 'let sleeping dogs lie,' and Bob no longer wanted to honor that agreement."

"It seems logical," I said, "except we don't have any proof of a change between them in recent weeks."

"It's a guess." Nonetheless, Captain Marshall jotted another note.

"An educated guess based on Bob's demand that Betty give up her charity work."

"It's possible the competition between the two men surfaced again."

Taking the marker in my, I wrote one more name on the board. "It's also possible Bob was making a more direct statement leading us to Larry Fox."

"Referring to his confrontation with Larry over the dog and the flower beds." The chief tapped his pen on the table.

"Maybe Bob left the 'sleeping dog' clue to direct Betty toward Larry as a suspect in the event of a mishap. Or, in this case, a murder."

When I stood back to survey the board, six names remained: Thomas Fisher, Bob Wilson, Betty Hamilton, Pete Scott, Larry Fox, and Alyssa Burney.

The chief pointed to two names with his pen. "Let's cross Thomas Fisher and Pete Scott off the list for now. They don't seem as closely connected to the case as the others."

I drew a bold line through their names.

"That leaves four suspects," I said.

"Four suspects with the motive, the means, and the opportunity. And, potentially, more than one murderer among them."

"What would you like me to do next?"

"Go home, Josie. I'll take it from here."

And I meant to do as he said. I really did. But something unexpected happened, to change my plans.

Chapter Twenty-Nine

I planned to do as the chief asked—and I would have—except that the exact moment I was getting into my car, my phone rang. It was Kate. She and her mom, Faith, urged me to meet them right away.

"We're parked down the block from Miss Betty's School of Dance. We saw Alyssa with Larry, dragging more boxes into her car. So, we stopped to talk to her."

"What?" I felt a flutter of fear at her words. "Kate, you need to be careful."

"No worries," she said, as if she hadn't engaged with a possible murderer—or two. "We told her she couldn't leave town without a 'going away' party."

"I don't believe you."

"Well, you'd better believe it. We're having it at your house an hour from now."

"What? We can't do that. I promised the chief I would go home and let him handle things from here."

"That's what I'm telling you." My friend's voice rang urgently over the phone. "You need to go home and get ready for the party. Alyssa is leaving early in the morning, so we must help her celebrate tonight. She actually seemed quite pleased that we would want to wish her well."

I sensed one of those little warning bells ringing in my head, but I couldn't figure out how to make it stop. "Okay. I'll go home and clean my bathroom. Who's coming to this party?"

"The mahjong ladies will be there. And Betty, of course."

"No 'dance moms' or little ballerinas?"

"No, silly. It's just a few women who want to help a young girl who's going back to school for the semester."

"Well, that's different." My sarcasm was lost on Kate. "What could possibly go wrong?"

Kate assured me the refreshments were handled. "You might want to pick up a bouquet of flowers or something. We'll bring food and party supplies, like always."

"Fine. I'll see you at my house in an hour."

"Better make it a half-hour. We have one other surprise for you, and I need to set it up."

"I don't even want to know about it."

"You'll love it."

"You've got my extra key. If you get there first, go on in."

"Oh, and Josie?"

"Yes."

"One more thing. Could you pick up Betty and bring her with you? She doesn't like to drive at night. I can take her home after the party."

"Why not?" I asked, resigned to doing whatever she requested. "Will there be anything else?"

"No, that's it," she said sweetly. "See you in thirty minutes."

I buckled my seat belt and headed toward the Garden Cart. Before Jill opened the shop, we'd been forced to travel twenty miles to the next village for all things floral—weddings and funerals, birthdays and anniversaries. Even our small hospital hadn't offered flowers in their gift shop until Jill arranged to stock a chilled floral case with fresh arrangements each day.

Jill smiled up at me as I walked in the door. "How nice to see you, Josie. Are you looking for something special?"

"Yes. I know it's late in the day, but I need a bouquet for a party. Guests will be arriving in about twenty minutes."

After I explained the occasion, Jill led me to a glass case in her back room. "I have two options for you. You could go with an arrangement of fresh daisies that might be perfect for your table." She motioned to a white container of bright, cheery flowers.

"Or?"

"Or you might consider something more dramatic, like a single rose in one of these elegant glass vases." She set a thirty-six-inch-tall glass vase on top of her counter. The shape was beautifully unique. "This one reminds me of a dancer in the spotlight. It's called an Eiffel Tower vase. I have several extra-long stemmed roses to choose from, so you can select your color."

"I'll take the rose vase. I can give it to Alyssa as a going-away gift."

We selected three delicate pink roses, opening their petals, and Jill arranged them in the vase. "Add more water when you get home."

The vase was carefully nestled into Piper's back seat as I drove to Betty's. "Hop in, my friend. We don't want to be late to the party I'm hosting."

She sank gracefully into my little car, tucking her long legs beneath her skirt in a way I would never be able to duplicate. We sailed through light traffic, going the back roads from her house to mine. Although we arrived on schedule, the Mahjong Mavens were there ahead of us. Nellie took me aside as soon as Betty and I entered the front door.

"I already tidied your bathroom," she whispered in my ear. "It was no problem. I moved your bathrobe to the bedroom and put out a fresh roll of toilet paper."

"Thank you." I hugged her. It was nice to have friends you could count on without asking.

My eyes traveled over to the beautifully displayed refreshments spread the length of my kitchen counter island. Then, I turned to see why everyone had stopped talking. There stood my friends in hushed anticipation, waiting for me to notice what was hanging so delicately over Grandma Molly's table. It was Harvey's heavenly chandelier, its candle-shaped lights bathing the room in a warm glow. I did a double take, and they all burst out laughing.

"It's for you, Josie," Kate said. "Nellie's husband, Tim, installed it while you were doing my errands."

A lump formed in my throat, and tears welled in my eyes.

"Harvey wanted to surprise you."

I grabbed a tissue and blew my nose, struggling to compose myself. "Well, you certainly fooled me. You had me running all over town while you invaded

156

my house to surprise me."

Sharon came over to give me a hug.

I couldn't stop smiling as I admired the beautiful gift. The chandelier was perfect in my dining room. I already imagined a festive holiday dinner with all my friends together. Then, I thought about how much time Harvey had spent designing and creating the chandelier. I shook my head and put my hands out in front of me.

"What is it?" Kate asked.

"It's too much. I can't possibly accept it." My eyes filled with tears as I realized the enormity of the gift.

"Josie Posey, when a gentleman wants to give you a well-deserved gift, you must accept it," Kate said. "Harvey would be crushed if you made us take it back down."

My circle of friends waited as I pondered Kate's words. Finally, I nodded. "Yes. I'm keeping it." A cumulative cheer exploded in the room, and all eyes turned back to Kate.

"Good. I'm glad that's settled," said Betty. "We've got one more celebration. I invited Alyssa here as a surprise send-off."

I walked closer to the refreshments and could see she had taken charge of the theme. All the paper plates and napkins had the same message: DANCE LIKE NO ONE IS WATCHING.

"Sharon, you are remarkable. This sentiment is probably better for me than it is for Alyssa. She will do fine with everyone watching."

Alyssa arrived to a warm welcome. We gathered around my grandmother's long table and shared stories while we nibbled on the snacks. Nellie poured wine, and the rest of us relaxed and enjoyed the evening. Kate was the first to ask Alyssa about her plans.

"I know you want to be a dancer. What is your plan to get into a ballet company?"

Alyssa glanced toward Betty before she answered. "I had hoped to go to a bigger city, but I don't think that's going to happen."

Betty wrapped an arm around the younger woman's shoulders. "Don't be so sure of that. I talked this afternoon with Helgi, the artistic director for the

San Francisco Ballet. He wants you to come there for tryouts next week."

Alyssa stood absolutely still, her face turning bright red as she struggled to contain her emotions. "Oh, Betty!" She burst into tears and rushed into the bathroom, sobbing behind the closed door.

"Well," Sharon said dryly, "I'm guessing those are happy tears, right?"

Betty followed Alyssa and knocked gently on the bathroom door. "Come join us. We're here to celebrate with you, not make you cry."

A few minutes later, we gathered around the table again, recalling our own college years and laughing. Alyssa remained quiet. Finally, she excused herself, claiming she had to finish packing for her trip. Harvey arrived as she was leaving.

"Is Alyssa okay?" he asked, pulling me aside. "She seems awfully subdued for a young girl headed off to chase her dreams."

"I think she's overwhelmed by it all." But, inside, I wondered.

The party ended soon after Alyssa left. Kate gave Betty a ride home. The others cleared the food away, and Harvey stayed behind. I thanked him for the beautiful chandelier, and we admired the light shimmering from its candelabra. "For Christmas Eve, I might replace the bulbs with candles."

"That would be perfect." Harvey's eyes glistened at the thought.

We sat on my couch, drinking wine, and talking about the success of the Summer's End Festival. I pondered how spending time with this man was always comfortable and easy.

"Are you planning to send some of your art to the gallery in the city?"

Harvey looked surprised. "What are you talking about?"

"The redheaded man at your booth, I thought I recognized him. Later, Nellie confirmed he owns a prestigious art gallery in Kansas City. He gave you his card, didn't he?"

"Oh, Josie, I don't think he meant for me to contact him," Harvey said. "He was being polite."

I turned toward him and put both of my hands on his. "Harvey, a businessman, doesn't give you his card if he doesn't expect you to call him. The guy loved your work. You need to get in touch with him this week."

Harvey shook his head. "You don't even know who he is."

"Oh yes, I do. His name is Finnigan O'Connor. He's related to the family that started O'Connor Greeting Cards in Kansas City. He is well-respected in the art world, and he's looking for new artists. He loves supporting talented people from our area."

"I see." Harvey grinned at me. "You've been doing your homework."

"I have. Promise me you'll give him a call."

Before he left, I thanked Harvey again for the chandelier. "I will always treasure it."

"I hope so. I designed it with this very spot in mind. I just didn't know it at the time."

He reminded me to lock the door and turn on the porch light as a final precaution for the evening.

"Do you really think that's necessary?" I asked incredulously. "The chief has Michael in custody. We're still figuring out the details, but he has practically confessed to the murder."

"Don't forget the chief's officers may still have orders to check on you. How would you like it if a SWAT team woke you in the wee hours of the morning just because you turned your light off?"

"Good point." I locked the door and turned on the front porch light as he left.

Chapter Thirty

I showered, then climbed into bed, deciding to read my book for a while. It had been a busy day, and I needed time to relax my mind. Bedtime was always my best opportunity for uninterrupted reading, so I chose a book from the stack of titles ready and waiting on my nightstand.

Before long, I realized I was reading the same line again and again. My eyelids were so heavy I could no longer keep them open. Moe slept soundly, and the rhythm of his snoring lulled me into a light doze. When my book collapsed on my chest, I woke up, startled.

I shook my head, remembering all the nights when I was a child and my mother had fallen asleep on our sofa. If I woke her, she always insisted she had been "resting her eyes." Now, I understood how she felt. One moment, I was resting my eyes; the next, I was fast asleep. I set aside my book and switched off the light.

The shrill ringing of my phone woke me again. It felt like my head had barely touched the pillow, but the clock on my nightstand told me it was straight-up midnight. I grabbed the phone, placing it to my ear. "This is Josie," I answered groggily.

I could hear Alyssa's voice shaking through her tears. "I need your help, Josie." The girl's voice broke as she said my name.

"What is it, Alyssa? Are you all right?"

"I don't know what to do," she cried. "I'm so sorry. I never meant to hurt anyone."

"What are you saying?" I kept my voice low and steady, hoping to calm the girl and keep her talking.

160

"Where are you? Let me come and get you, so we can talk."

"I'm at the dance studio. Please come. I have to tell you the whole story."

"I'll be there in ten minutes." I disconnected and dialed Chief Marshall before racing to the studio. We arrived at the same time. Officer Devon pulled in behind us.

A single light led us to the cozy office at the back of the studio. Alyssa was curled into an oversized leather chair, her bright pink dance bag at her feet. She wore yoga pants and a T-shirt that proclaimed: I LOVE TO DANCE. She held a soft cloth ballerina doll who wore pink ballet slippers with ribbons laced up her legs. My heart broke for her. She looked about twelve instead of twenty.

I sat on the ottoman to be near her. The chief took the desk chair, and Officer Devon stood against the wall next to the door.

Alyssa wiped tears from her face. "Betty gave me this doll. She told me every dancer should have a ballet doll on her pillow and a ballerina jewelry box on her dresser. She was always so good to me…and now she will hate me forever."

"I'm sure she won't hate you." I reached out to reassure the girl.

"Oh, yes, she will. I'm responsible for Bob's death. Betty will never forgive me."

My hands flew to my mouth, and I shot a look at the chief. Alyssa sobbed as she told her story, which came out in clipped sentences.

"I wanted to audition for a big ballet company, and Betty wasn't helping. And Michael said some flowers were editable, but not the belladonna. Then Larry said I should do something about it 'cause I deserved a chance."

Now Alyssa had the hiccups. Her shoulders heaved, and I could barely understand her rambling confession.

"The flowers looked just like dancers on their toes," she sobbed. "B..B… Betty told me to take all I wanted, and I picked a whole basket. For a huge bouquet."

Chief Marshall handed the girl a tissue.

She wiped her nose and kept talking. "Then my brother said, 'let's teach Bob a lesson with his own flowers.'"

We waited while Alyssa dabbed at her eyes and nose again. She took a deep breath. "And he took my bouquet. And he brought me a jar of petal powder. And I put it in Bob's salsa. And now he's dead."

She shrank into her chair and sniffled.

The chief handed her another tissue. "Do you still have the jar from the powder?"

She nodded and pointed to the dance bag beside her.

"Where is your brother?"

Before she could answer, the exterior door slammed, and Larry ran down the hall, sneakers slapping on the tile all the way to the office. We heard him yell as he ran. "Alyssa. Alyssa. Don't tell them anything. You hear me?"

He crashed into the room and raced to her side. The sneakers squealed as he cut across the floor. She looked up at him, tears streaming down her face.

"I had to," she hiccupped.

"No!" Larry screamed. "Where is it?" He looked wildly around the room.

When Alyssa's eyes slid to the bright pink dance bag, Larry made a dive for it. His elbow smacked my face with such force that he knocked me off the ottoman. The chief leaped to his feet and rounded the desk. I scrambled to my knees and grabbed for the bag. Neither of us was quick enough. Larry whipped the bag out of my hands. He slung it over his shoulder and bolted for the door.

Officer Devon stood in the way, feet planted, gun drawn. Larry slid to a stop, still clutching the pink bag.

"Don't test me," Devon said.

Larry wailed like a wounded animal. He dropped to the floor and held the bag to his chest. "We didn't do anything wrong," he whimpered.

Devon knelt to fasten handcuffs around Larry's wrists while the chief cuffed Alyssa.

"Let's get them both to the station," the chief ordered. "Keep 'em separated."

He motioned for me to follow them, and the five of us walked out the door together.

Alyssa sat in the interrogation room with her eyes lowered, her tightly cuffed hands clasped on the table in front of her. I watched from the end of the table, holding an ice pack against my right eye and the bridge of my nose, while the chief repeated Alyssa's Miranda rights and flipped on the tape recorder.

"You know we have a confession from Michael Wilson, don't you, Alyssa?"

"I know." She blew her nose into a tissue. "He didn't do anything, though. Except to answer Larry's questions about the potency of the Naked Lady flowers."

"Did he assist you in any way?"

"Well, yeah. He was great. He talked to Larry about his allergies. He said it was probably the pollen and that some people made their own antigens out of freeze-dried flowers. Even showed him how the machine worked."

"I meant, did he help you murder Bob?" the chief said.

"Larry?"

"Michael," the chief said. "Did Michael Wilson help you poison Bob Hamilton?"

"Oh." Alyssa thought before she answered. "He told Larry about poisonous flowers. And how easy it was to grind the dried blossoms into powder."

"But did Michael know you planned to harm Bob?"

Alyssa rolled her eyes. "We didn't plan to hurt him. We only wanted to make him sick."

The chief shot me a glance. I shrugged my shoulders in sympathy, but my face hurt too much to smile.

"Alyssa," the chief began again, "What did Michael know about your plan to make Bob sick?"

"Ahh," the light went on in Alyssa's eyes. "Nothing. Michael didn't know about the argument Larry had with Mr. Hamilton. He didn't know I was mad at Betty. We didn't tell anyone about The Big Plan."

"All he knew was that Larry wanted to protect the dogs he walked—to keep them safe. My brother called Michael Wilson once to talk to him about all kinds of plants. The Naked Lady flowers were on his list."

"Mr. Wilson had nothing to do with your decision to poison Bob Hamilton?" the chief repeated the question.

"No." Alyssa shook her head firmly.

After Alyssa finished, the chief led her from the interrogation room and returned to me.

"We've been holding Michael in a jail cell long enough. Let's clear up the confusion now. I want to be certain he wasn't involved in the murder. It's still possible he helped with the formula for the high-powered poison."

I shook my head. "I don't think so, Chief. He was ready to take the blame, but he had no reason to protect Alyssa or her brother."

"Let's hope you're right," he said.

We walked down the hall to the rear of the station and paused at the cell door. The chief gave me an encouraging nod. "Follow my lead, Josie."

He rapped sharply to awaken Michael Wilson. Then, he unlocked the door, and we stepped inside. Michael rubbed his eyes and looked up at us.

"What happened to your face?" He stared at my swollen nose and blackening eye.

"You should see the other guy," I quipped.

"We need to talk." The chief turned on the light, and Michael sat up, swinging his legs onto the floor to perch on the edge of the cot.

"It's the middle of the night," Michael said. "Can't it wait?"

"Now." The chief's voice was firm. Michael shrugged and slid his feet into his loafers. The three of us gathered in the small conference room where so many important conversations had taken place.

"Mr. Wilson, you led us to believe that you killed Mr. Hamilton, and we now feel certain you lied about your involvement," said Chief Marshall.

I watched as the blood drained from Michael's face. Stunned, he placed his folded hands on the table and looked up at us. "Did she confess?"

"Yes," the chief said. "We will file formal charges against her this morning."

"I was afraid you would find out. She talked to me a few weeks ago, and I could see she was desperate. She wanted to go to New York, and she didn't see any way to get there."

At this point, I couldn't tell whether he was referring to the ballerina or her assistant. Both wanted to go to New York. I prompted Michael to continue. "You were trying to help her make that happen?"

"I feared she had taken matters into her own hands. I didn't believe she would kill anyone, but I knew she would try to get attention by taking drastic action."

"By poisoning him?"

"I didn't know. I figured if she had killed him, she couldn't survive the consequences on her own. She isn't strong enough. So, I confessed for her. What will happen to her?" Sadness claimed his face.

The chief responded. "She will need an attorney. Then, she may attempt to get her charges reduced from murder to involuntary manslaughter. That's a legal matter out of my control."

"If they find her guilty, how long could she be in prison?"

"That depends. The range could be from five to twenty years. But she's young, so she would still have a full life ahead of her."

Michael raised his hands to his head in anguish. "What are you talking about? Betty is thirty-two. She could be in her fifties by the time she is released."

The chief looked at me and nodded. "Just as you suspected, Josie."

I looked sympathetically at the confused man in front of me. "You thought Betty killed Bob, didn't you? So, you confessed to save her life."

"Yes. That's what I just told you." His eyes filled with tears. "Betty was so angry with Bob I was certain she did it. I never asked her, of course. I didn't want to accuse her."

"But you did want to protect her."

Michael held his head high. "I would do anything for her."

"The good news is you won't have to." I smiled at him.

"What are you saying?" Michael stared at us, a puzzled look on his face.

"She didn't do it."

"What? If Betty didn't kill Bob, who did?"

"We have a new person of interest." I turned to the chief with a grin on my swollen face.

Chief Marshall stood and walked toward the door. "Mr. Wilson, you've caused us a great deal of extra work. If you had simply told the truth, we might have solved this case earlier. As it is, you could still be charged with obstruction of justice."

He opened the door. "Now, collect your personal effects and get out of my police station. And if you see Betty, tell her I will call later in the day to brief her on new developments in her husband's murder case."

Michael smiled. "I'll do that."

Chapter Thirty-One

L arry sat across from me in the now-familiar interrogation room, his eyes avoiding mine.

The dog walker raised his head to look at me. "Sorry, Ms. Posey."

"You're apologizing to *me*?"

"Yeah. I feel awful bad about that phone call, the day I took Moe for a walk. I was only trying to scare you a little."

"Mission accomplished." I clasped my hands on the table and waited.

"And I'm sorry I knocked you down." He motioned to my bruised eye, which was worse this morning than it had been immediately after we tangled for Alyssa's dance bag.

The chief cleared his throat and turned on his tape recorder.

"What do you want to know?" Larry faced the chief. "We never meant to hurt Mr. Hamilton, but I guess we did."

"The man is dead, Larry."

"Well, it isn't our fault. He was such a jerk, yelling at the dog for nibbling on his flowers. And then Betty refused to help Alyssa get the internship she wanted."

"So, you decided to kill him? That was The Big Plan?" The chief glared at him across the table.

"Nah." Larry spread his hands out in denial. "We thought—well, I thought—that if Mr. Hamilton got sick, Betty would need to take care of him. Then, she would turn more over to Alyssa. I figured after Alyssa helped Betty with the studio and with taking care of Bob, Betty would be grateful."

"Grateful enough to give her the recommendation she wanted?" I looked into his eyes.

Larry shrugged. "Yeah." His head dropped. "I freeze-dried those Naked Lady flowers in my lab at the clock shop and ground them into powder. Alyssa mixed the poison into her brownies."

"I thought she put it in his salsa."

"Only after the brownies didn't make him sick. That's when I figured we needed to give him a little more, to make an impact."

"I'd say you made an impact," the chief said.

"We knew you would figure out that Mr. Hamilton got sick from the flowers. But we hoped you would think he spent too much time handling them without gloves. He was always out there pruning and weeding."

"You thought our investigation would lead to the conclusion that he accidentally killed himself by spending time in his flower garden?" The chief raised his eyebrows and looked directly at Larry.

"Maybe." Larry gave him a defiant look. "It could happen."

The chief shook his head. "You're going to have to come up with something better than that for your defense attorney. The two of you will be in jail for a long time."

He turned back to me. "I'll take it from here, Josie. Why don't you get some rest?"

I took one final look at Larry before I walked out of the room. The chief followed me into the hallway and closed the door on our murderer.

"Thank you for your help with the investigation," he said.

Then he paused.

"And thank your biddies, too."

"Ha ha. You can call us mavens."

Back at my cottage, I caught up on my reading while Moe settled comfortably on the floor beside the couch. Minutes into the book, I dozed off.

When my cell rang, I reached for it, accidentally knocking it to the floor. I grabbed it and answered with a halfhearted "Hello?"

Harvey's warm voice apologized immediately. "Oh no. I woke you."

"It's okay. Just dozed off while reading. Anyway, I'm going to Sharon's this afternoon, so I need to get up."

"Sounds like you had a late night."

"We arrested the real murderer."

"It wasn't Michael Wilson after all?"

"No. Not even close."

"That's good news." Harvey's voice was warm in my ear. "I called to see if you'd like to go to dinner with me. Maybe you could tell me all about it." I was silent for too long, causing him to consider my unspoken words. "It doesn't have to be a date." He said quickly. "I'd like to try out the new barbecue place the pastor's brother opened. I hoped you would go with me."

"I love barbecue."

"Tonight, at seven?"

"Sounds good," I said, smiling into the phone. "See you then."

The sweet fragrance of brown sugar and butter greeted me at Sharon's front door. I had no idea what she was baking, but I couldn't wait to taste it.

"Hello, ladies," I called out as I walked into her sunny kitchen.

Sharon was the first to spot my black eye and swollen nose. "Oh, Josie. Did someone punch you in the face?" Kate and Nellie gathered for a closer look.

I waved them away. "It was an accident," I said. "Long story. I'll tell you about it while we play."

My friend pulled a bag of peas from her freezer and slapped it against my face. "Hold this," she said.

"Is that a peach pie in your oven?" I changed the topic.

"Not this time. I promised you a new treat, and it's almost ready." She opened the oven door, and the sweet aroma filled the room.

"Is it your own recipe?" Kate peeked over Sharon's shoulder.

Sharon handed her an index card with handwritten instructions. "See what you think."

Tapping on her water glass for attention, Kate hushed everyone. "Ladies, today our own baker extraordinaire, Sharon Fitzpatrick, has prepared a remarkable new dessert."

"Hurry up, Kate," Nellie interrupted, "the suspense is killing us."

Kate directed her gaze toward me. "And this dessert looks like it's to die for."

Sharon took the card from Kate's hand. "Enough drama. The new dessert is Grandma Fitzpatrick's Peach Blueberry Crisp, and you are going to love it. At least, I hope you will. I haven't made it before, so you are standing in my test kitchen. You ladies will decide whether I should include it in my dessert menu for the Philbrook Bed and Breakfast."

"I don't need to know the ingredients," Kate said, lifting her nose into the air. "It smells wonderful, and it's coming out of your oven. I know it will be delicious."

"It's Terry's mother's recipe. It was the first dessert she made for us after we started dating. We can try my version in about an hour when it cools."

"Anyone ready to play mahjong?" Nellie poured the tiles onto the table.

"Yes." A chorus of voices answered. Together, we mixed the tiles and built two-tiered walls along the racks that formed a square to define the playing area.

"I'm East." Sharon claimed the opening position at the table and rolled the dice.

"Look. Doubles." Kate pointed to the pair of sixes Sharon rolled. "Anytime you have Sharon's dessert and roll doubles, it's going to be a good day."

"I have something to share with you," I said to the smiling ladies around me. "There have been new developments in the murder case."

"Good grief." Kate threw her hands in the air. "I thought you solved it already. Didn't Michael Wilson confess?"

"He did. But he confessed because he wanted to protect Betty."

"Betty did it?" Nellie asked sadly.

"Nope," I said with a dramatic pause. "It was Alyssa and her brother, Larry."

"I knew it." Kate clapped her hands.

Sharon cleared her throat. "Are we going to talk, or are we going to play?"

I had drawn my first tile when my cell phone rang. The table erupted in a collective sigh,

"Sorry, Ladies. I'll turn it off now."

Kate rearranged the tiles on the rack in front of her and leveled a glance in my direction. "Do it, Josie. This is a no-phone zone."

Nellie nodded her agreement, "We might be interested in murders the rest of the week, but it's mahjong on Wednesdays."

SHARON'S PERFECT PEACH PIE

- 1 double crust pie dough (recipe to follow)
- 6 cups sliced frozen peaches, thawed or fresh peaches skin removed and sliced
- 1/4 cup white sugar
- 1/4 cup brown sugar
- 1/4 cup all-purpose flour or 2 tablespoons quick-cooking tapioca
- 1/2 teaspoon cinnamon
- 1–2 tablespoons unsalted butter

1. Preheat the oven to 450 degrees. Line a baking sheet with foil or parchment paper.
2. Combine peaches, sugars, flour or tapioca, and cinnamon. Gently toss and set aside to juice up. Meanwhile, roll out chilled pie dough and turn out into a 9" pie plate. Fill with fruit and dot with butter. Place in the refrigerator and roll out pie dough. Top pie, crimp edges, and vent top. Alternatively, you can create a lattice top.
3. Mix 1 tablespoon of water with 1 egg yolk and brush on crust.
4. Place pie on a prepared tray and bake for 10 minutes. Reduce heat to 350 degrees and bake an additional 35–40 minutes or until the crust is golden and the pie is bubbly.

Double Pie Crust

- 2 1/2 cups all-purpose flour
- 1 1/2 teaspoons sugar

- 1 teaspoon salt
- 1/2 cup very cold butter, cut in small cubes
- 1/2 cup very cold lard (or Crisco), cut in small cubes
- 5 tablespoons ice-cold water (or more)

In a food processor combine flour, sugar, and salt, then pulse to combine. Add butter and lard and pulse until mixture resembles coarse meal. Transfer to a large bowl and with a fork, toss with water until dough begins to clump. With hands, gather dough together, divide in half and press into disc shape. Wrap in plastic and chill for at least 1 hour. Before rolling, soften slightly at room temp (5–10 minutes).

GRANDMA FITZPATRICK'S PEACH BLUEBERRY CRISP

- 4 cups sliced peaches (no need to peel)
- 1 cup blueberries
- Topping
- 1/2 cup all-purpose flour
- 1/2 cup packed brown sugar
- 1/4 cup unsalted butter
- 1/2 teaspoon salt
- 1/2 teaspoon cinnamon
- Grease a 9x13 pan with vegetable spray or butter. Put sliced peaches in a pan and sprinkle with blueberries.

For the topping:

In a separate bowl, combine dry ingredients. Cut in butter with a pastry blender until crumbly but not oily. Spread on top of fruit. Bake for 30 minutes. Serve warm with an optional scoop of vanilla ice cream.

NELLIE'S DENVER CASSEROLE

- 2 pounds ground round
- 2 tablespoons olive oil
- 1 small yellow onion, chopped
- 1 package sliced mushrooms (8 ounces)
- 1 teaspoon marjoram
- salt and pepper to taste

Sauté onions and mushrooms in olive oil until soft. Add hamburger and cook until browned. Add seasonings.

Add:

- 1 can stewed tomatoes (run through food processor)
- 1 can tomato soup
- 1 teaspoon Italian herbs
- Pour over the meat and simmer for 15 minutes.

While that simmers, cook a 12-ounce package of egg noodles (Reames Homestyle Egg Noodles or similar).

Alternating layers: sauce, noodles, and Velveeta cheese slices.

Bake at 350 degrees F for 30 minutes.

BARBARA'S CHEESY PLEASY PUPPY SCONES

(for pets only)

- 1 cup all-purpose flour
- 2 teaspoons baking powder
- 1/4 cup olive oil
- 1 cup grated light cheddar cheese
- 1/2 cup diced cooked chicken
- 1/2 cup plus 2 tablespoons skim milk
- 1/4 cup bacon crumbles (2–3 strips of bacon, cooked to crispy, and crumbled)

Preheat the oven to 400 degrees. Grease a baking sheet with nonstick vegetable spray.

Stir together the flour and baking powder in a large bowl. Pour the olive oil into the flour mixture and stir until thoroughly blended. Stir in the cheese and chicken. Add ½ cup milk to make a soft dough.

Turn the dough out onto a lightly floured surface and knead gently until smooth. With a rolling pin, roll the dough out to a ¾-inch thickness.

Cut into 2-inch rounds with a cookie cutter or glass, and place on the baking sheet. Brush each biscuit with the remaining milk and bake for 17 to 20 minutes, or until the cheese bits begin to bubble and lightly brown. Remove from the oven and sprinkle with finely ground bacon crumbles.

Cool to room temperature before serving.

Store in an airtight container for up to 5 days. Or, wrap wet and freeze for up to 2 months. (Thaw before serving.)

Makes 12 scones.

K-STATE'S SKUNK ODOR REMOVAL SOLUTION

- 1 quart 3% hydrogen peroxide
- 1/4 cup baking soda
- 1 teaspoon liquid soap

Acknowledgements

Thank you for reading *Doomed by Blooms*, and continuing this far. I hope you've had as much fun solving this mystery as I did writing it.

My sincere appreciation goes to the writers and editors who guided me in the development of this book. This includes the generous friends in Pitch to Published, Sisters in Crime, Mystery Writers of America, Pitch Perfect, and others. (Kathy VerEecke, this wouldn't have happened without you.) I am also indebted to the "accountability" support team from our NANOWRIMO writers. Your encouragement–or was it nagging?—never wavered. You know who you are.

"Thank You" isn't enough to express my gratitude to the readers and editors who made me a better writer—cozy writer Andi Cumbo, the brilliant editor Patrick Price, and my author friends Jane, Harriett, Paula, and Amber, among others. I would be honored to have my book sitting on a shelf beside any of yours.

A huge thank you to my fabulous agent, Cindy Bullard, of Birch Literary, who believed in my writing enough to take me under her wing. Her incredible editing skills made *Doomed by Blooms* a better book (especially the ending), and her enthusiasm sold it to the amazing Shawn Reilly Simmons at Level Best Books.

To Shawn and the other talented Dames of Detection at LBB—Verena Rose and Harriette Sackler—thank you for your knowledge, your patience and your dedication to making dreams come true for debut authors like me. I am so grateful to be among the talented writers you represent.

Many thanks to Lyndsey Mbwauike, for the design that inspired the book cover, and to Shawn Reilly Simmons for bringing the cover art to life.

Sometimes, friends are so close they qualify as family. My gratitude goes to those who traveled this writing journey along with me. Hugs to Sharon, Janet, and Jane, who first learned of cozy mysteries when I announced my plans to write one. To Jodi, Marlynn, Karen and Bob for their unwavering encouragement. And, especially to the real Mah Jongg Mavens, who may see themselves in this story—Susan, Karen, June, Cheri, Carolyn, and Jane.

I owe many thanks to those who contributed to the content of this story. I'm grateful to Barbara Chamberlin, who allowed me to use her real name and her dog biscuit recipe. Thank you to Karen Townsley for sharing her Perfect Peach Pie recipe, and to Susan Neff for providing Nellie's Denver Casserole. And to the family of Les Anderson, who approved my unorthodox tribute to his memory through a female character bearing his name, I will be forever grateful to have called Les my friend. To the veterinarians at Kansas State University, thanks for the skunk odor recipe. Finally, thank you to my family–sisters Jan and Ann, aunts and cousins, nieces, and nephews. (Yes, Martha, Winona and Jeneva, Andi and Abby this includes you.)

A special thank you to Teresa, sister of my heart, for saying "yes" even when I ask you to read a messy first draft. I'm so lucky to have you.

To our sweet, funny Old English sheepdog, Oliver, thank you for serving as a role model for Moe and for listening to me when I read chapters aloud. You are the best assistant a writer could have.

Finally, I'm truly grateful to be surrounded by the ones I love most of all: Bruce, who has always made me smile. Our son Matthew (and his beautiful wife Tatiya). Our son Zachary. And especially our grandson Zander and granddaughter Madeline, who own my heart.

About the Author

Anna St. John is a former newspaper journalist, award-winning advertising copywriter, and ad agency owner. She lives in a small Kansas town with a working blacksmith shop, much like the one in this story. Anna is a member of Mystery Writers of America, Sisters in Crime, the Kansas Authors Club and the National Mah Jongg League.

SOCIAL MEDIA HANDLES:
    Facebook: https://www.facebook.com/cozyauthor/
    Website: https://www.anna-stjohn.com/
    Twitter: @AuthorStJohn

AUTHOR WEBSITE:
    Anna-StJohn.com
    Author email: author.anna.stjohn@gmail.com